SAFE

Kate Hanney

Second Edition
Published in 2013 by Applecore Books
www.applecorebooks.co.uk

A CIP catalogue record for this title is available from
the British Library.

A Note From The Author

For the last fifteen years I've worked as an English teacher in South Yorkshire, and by doing this job I've had the privilege of meeting hundreds of fantastic kids. Some are comedians and some are geniuses. At times, some of them are desperately unhappy, and one or two of them are just plain scary!

But they all have a story to tell, and that's what this is – it's a story about a boy.

To D Jeffery

It would've never been finished
without your kind words
and encouragement.
Cheers, love.

ONE

The day of Chris's party had been shit. I'd had a row at home, isolation at school, no bus fare and no fags. I should've known it was the wrong day to take a chance with the pregnancy thing. My luck was bang out.

I'd only gone to school in the first place to get the 'Education Welfare Officer' off my back. He'd been round to the house again, acting all serious and talking about legal action. At first, I was going to ignore him like usual, but my mom got the face on, and I thought the best way to keep them both happy was to just turn up every now and again. So the next morning, I went.

It was all OK until French. I hated French – oh I know everybody does – but I really couldn't stand it. Our usual teacher wasn't too bad with me though. She, like most of the others, sort of knew I wasn't going to do much because I didn't see the point.

I was never going to be a brain surgeon was I? And I really didn't see what difference a couple of GCSEs were going to make to my life. She understood this, and she pretty much left me alone. But that

5

exams

Friday we had a cover teacher. I knew him a bit, he'd been in some of our lessons before; but he didn't know me, not well enough to realise when to back off anyway.

It started from the minute I walked through the door. It was the second lesson of the day, and we didn't have a break between that and the first. So it was always a bit difficult: leaving lesson one, trying to get twos on a fag, and then not being late for the next lesson. Well I was a bit late that day, only a couple of minutes, but it was enough to wind him up.

'What's your name?' he snapped.

I told him, and he made the 'Ah' sound. The 'Ah' meant he recognised my name; he knew then that I was one of those lads who hardly ever attended, and when I did, I always managed to get my name on the detention list. He shook his head and sighed; the look on his face was that dirty, he'd need bleach to get it off. *exagurate*

'Well, what do you think you're playing at, turning up at this time?' *—moody*

He was being right mardy, and he didn't give me chance to answer the first question before he went babbling on with the next.

'Who do you think you are, blah, blah, blah ... disturbing the lesson, blah, blah ...

you'll make the time up at break, blah, blah, blah.'

OK, OK, I thought, staying calm. It's only a couple of minutes, I can put up with that. I tried hard to ignore him and made my way to an empty chair at the back.

The next thing though, it was my jacket. We're not supposed to wear coats during the lessons, but it was freezing in that classroom and I only had a T-shirt on underneath. Sometimes I could get away with leaving it on. But not that day; Mr Supply Teacher was going to follow the rules to the letter.

'Remove your coat as well,' he shouted, before I'd even sat down.

'OK, give me a chance,' I said.

'Don't speak to me like that! Just do it!'

I don' know why he had to be all cocky and over the top, but I decided to let him. I preferred to keep quiet if I could, so I sat down and took my jacket off. The cold made me shiver.

He put some worksheets in front of me and walked away. They weren't hard and I could probably have had a go at them. But I didn't, because I hadn't brought a pen. Now let's face it, I had all on getting myself up on time, putting on something that resembled school uniform, getting my little sister up, getting her to school, then getting me to school and finding out where I should be, without remembering to bring a pen as well. I knew I didn't have one, I never did, but because he'd had a go at me twice in two minutes, I thought I'd wait and see what happened; sometimes, cover teachers never even got up from sitting behind the desk.

I sat and looked out of the window for a bit. Some of the girls were on the field doing P.E. and it was quite entertaining. I knew a few of them well and the memories made me smile – but not for long. Unfortunately, the muppet at the front must've felt like a walk round, and all at once, there he was, standing in front of me.

'You've done absolutely nothing. You've been sitting there all this time and you haven't written a single word.'

I looked at him.

'What's a matter with you, lad, why haven't done anything?'

'I haven't got a pen,' I answered.

Now normally, the teachers would tut and shake their heads a bit when this happened. But then, they'd just go and get me a pen and I'd make an effort to do some work. But this idiot, he decided he was going to make a big deal about it.

'Oh he hasn't got a pen,' he shouted, all dramatic, waving his hands in the air. 'Well, perhaps if you sit there long enough, one will fly in through the window and land straight in your hand.' He looked around at the other kids, pleased with himself. Maybe he thought he'd get a laugh, that they'd be impressed with his wit. Funny

But most of them weren't even listening, and the ones who were didn't have a clue what he was on about.

I just glared at him. I hated people being sarcastic anyway, but from a teacher, it really did my head in. I mean, there was no need for it. Why couldn't he just say "Well you should've asked for one earlier"? And then he would've been right, and I wouldn't have argued. Why did he have to make it into an event? Why did he try to show me up and make me look stupid?

I shook my head. 'You sad bastard.'

I sighed out my thoughts almost under my breath. And it was the almost that got me into trouble; a bit quieter and he wouldn't have heard. But he did, and he threw a right strop.

'What did you say?'

Oh God, here we go. 'Nothing,' I said. I just didn't feel like arguing.

'Yes you did, I heard you. Now come on, if you're big enough to say it in the first place then at least be brave enough to admit it.'

He was proper shouting now; acting all hard and pushing and pushing me, more and more. All the other kids had gone quiet and they were all looking at me; I could feel my stomach getting tight. I really hadn't wanted any trouble, but he just wouldn't leave it alone.

'Well, I'm waiting. Or aren't you so clever now?'

He obviously thought I was keeping quiet because I was scared of him, and that must've made him feel good.

He came right up to my desk and leaned over, really near to my face. 'Not so brave when you've got to say it out loud, are you? Well you're pathetic, lad. Absolutely pathetic ... aren't you?'

As he shouted out his high and mighty opinions, I felt some of his spit land on my lips, and then I just couldn't hold it in any longer. It was right what I'd said anyway, he'd just proved it, right there in front of all the other kids.

'I said you're a sad bastard.' I didn't shout, but I said it plenty loud enough and I looked straight at him as I spoke.

10

He stood bolt upright then with a shocked look on his face. That had thrown him. He really hadn't expected that; he probably thought I was going to agree with him, or apologise or something. Because I hadn't said anything for so long, he thought he'd won his little battle and made me look stupid and pathetic or whatever it was he was trying to do.

He didn't know what to say then though, so he did what they always do in that situation – he pointed at the door and screamed, 'Get out!'

But as he stood there with his arm stretched out, I could see his hand was shaking. paused

I hesitated for a second. I could've had a real go at him then, like I would've done when I was younger. I could have told him about himself or threatened him or even thrown a few things. But I'd shaken him up alright and that was enough.

And I knew I'd be going into isolation for what I'd done already. So although I was really wound up, I kept my mouth shut. I'd made my point and so I did what I was told. I stood up, got my jacket and walked out of the room.

Outside in the corridor, I threw myself back against the wall hard. I swore a few times, and thought about what I'd like to do to him. But then I tried to calm myself down. I'd learned the benefit of doing that a long time ago. They liked to see that you could sort yourself out a bit, 'Anger Management' they called it.

I closed my eyes for a second and took a few deep breaths. After a while, my heart started to beat slower. Control

One of the girls came out of the classroom with an orange piece of paper in her hand. This was a sort of form thing that the teachers filled in when somebody had kicked off and they wanted them dealing with. They wrote down what had happened and then they got a 'good kid' to take it to the office.

This 'good kid' was called Mel. I didn't know her that well, but as she walked past she looked at me. It was a strange look; one that I couldn't quite work out.

It wasn't the 'you low-down piece of crap' look that I would've expected from her. It was a sort of smile, and it was enough to make my eyes follow her all the way down the corridor.

When she'd gone out of sight, I thought about what'd happened again and I almost went home – it wouldn't have been the first time I'd walked out of school. But then I saw old Rogers coming towards me with the orange form in his hand. Mr Rogers was the deputy head, and to be honest, we'd always got on OK. The only run-ins we had were at times like this, when somebody else had wound me up and he had to deal with it.

'Oh, Danny, not again.' These were his first words as he stopped and stood next to me. He looked quite mad. 'It's really not on! You can't just go on saying these things. You know you should bring a pen, and if you don't, you should ask to borrow one properly. You know that, don't you?'

As well as looking mad, he seemed disappointed, and I nearly felt a bit bad then. What he'd said so far was true, what could I say? I looked across the corridor and out of the window. 'Yes, sir,' I said, and he carried on.

'You can't just start swearing and causing trouble like this. I've told you before.' He paused for a minute, then said, 'There was no need for this to have happened, was there?'

I didn't answer.

'Was there, Danny?'

His voice had got louder and I turned my head back to look at him. I wanted to tell him then, I wanted to tell him how it'd all been his fault, Mr what-ever his name was – if he hadn't tried to show me up and make me look thick in the first place, and then if he'd have just left me alone, I mean, he'd kept asking me what I'd said, hadn't he? He'd pushed me into repeating it, going on and on and on.

But what was the point? It wouldn't have done me any good anyway; they always stuck together in the end.

So I cut my losses, 'No, sir,' I said quietly.

I thought he was going to tell me to apologise then, but he didn't; maybe he could tell it wasn't the best time. There was no way I would've said sorry then anyway, no chance. But he knew if he left me alone for a bit, I'd be more likely to do what he said.

'Right; good,' he nodded. 'Now, come with me up to the PRU.'

I followed him all the way along the corridor and up the stairs.

Our isolation unit was foul. I mean I know it wasn't supposed to be a holiday camp or anything, but it was the most depressing place in the world. When I first started at that school, it was always called 'Isolation', but then a couple of years ago somebody decided it should be called a

Pupil Referral Unit or 'PRU.' That sounded much more friendly, didn't it?

Well it wasn't. It was exactly the same as it always had been; sub-zero temperatures and boring as hell.

It was an old classroom that had been split up into what they called 'bases,' and when we got there, Rogers told me which one to sit in. As I flopped down, the teacher who ran it looked at me and nearly said something. Maybe she was going to tell me to take my coat off or something, I don't know, because she quickly changed her mind and said nothing. She'd known me for a while and could tell I was pissed off. She decided to leave me alone.

Rogers told me that I had to spend the rest of the day there, but if I behaved myself, I could go back into normal lessons on Monday.

'But,' he said seriously. 'This is getting far too regular, Danny. If it happens again, you'll be looking at another exclusion.'

I frowned – didn't he realise that an exclusion would suit me down to the ground? It would give me a real, proper reason for not going to school.

He cottoned on to what I was thinking and he couldn't help smiling. 'Just try not to do it again, Danny, eh; it's better for everybody. OK?'

I nodded and he went.

Bastard supply teacher, I thought, as the door closed, and I put my hood up, got my key out of my pocket and started carving into the desk.

TWO

The four and a half hours I spent in isolation that day seemed more like four and a half weeks. It was sooo boring. And then on top of that, when I got let out at three o'clock, I realised I hadn't got enough money for bus fare. There was a loan system set up at our school for this sort of thing, but you couldn't use it if you already owed money – and of course, I already did.

So there was nothing I could do; just zip up my jacket and start walking.

After the long hike home, I was icy cold, and when I walked into our house there didn't seem to be any rise in the temperature. Nobody was home, which wasn't unusual. But our dog, Tyson, went bonkers when I went in through the front door; at least somebody was pleased to see me.

I went into the kitchen and started looking around for something to eat. All the fridge had to offer was eight cans of lager, a two litre bottle of Coke and some cheese that didn't smell too good.

The cupboards were a bit more promising: soup, baked beans and chip-shop-style mushy peas. That wasn't bad. I began to plan my tea, but it all depended on bread. Was there any? I reached up and opened the cupboard ... Yes! Half a loaf. That must've been my slice of good luck for the day.

Anyway, beans on toast. That would do fine; nice and quick and warm.

The plates were all dirty and piled up at the side of the sink. I chose the one that looked least scummy, washed it under the tap and got on with making my tea.

When it was ready I took it into the living room. I turned on the television and sank down into the deep dip in the settee. Tyson had followed me, and he sat watching every mouthful I ate. The programme on TV was that one where the chefs have to make a meal out of just a few ingredients. Ha, I thought to myself – I'd like to see what they could come up with out of our kitchen!

The beans were almost finished when I heard my mom's key in the door and she walked in. 'Hello, love.'

Love, I thought; she's in a good mood.

'Lacey upstairs?' she asked.

Oh God. My stomach did a somersault and my eyes got wide. I was meant to pick up my little sister from her primary school on my way home. I had totally forgotten. It was getting put in isolation that'd done it – anybody's mind would've gone dead in there.

My mom read the look on my face and immediately went mental. 'I don't believe it, not again. What's up with you? It was the last thing I said to you before you took her to school this morning. Don't forget to pick her up, I said. Those teachers already think I'm useless ...'

I tried to get an excuse in but she was off again, shaking her head and really laying into me. 'For God's sake, can't you do anything right? She could be anywhere by now. Not that you'd care, you selfish little sod. You don't care about anybody except yourself.'

I thought about Lacey waiting for me at school and me not turning up, and for a couple of seconds I felt sick. But then I thought about it again, and this time I felt mad instead. I mean, why should I have to pick Lacey up anyway? Why should I be the one feeling guilty?

Normally, I would've argued back with my mom and asked all this. Sometimes we had real shouting matches and said foul things to each other.

But this time, after I'd stared at her for a few seconds, I decided to leave it. She had tears in her eyes and her hands were shaking as she rummaged around in her pockets for a cigarette and a lighter. I almost apologised, then didn't. I didn't really do apologies as a rule, not unless it was to get me out of isolation at school; I could sometimes manage one then, but it was just words.

I sat back and fixed my eyes on the television. Leave her to it; let her have her moment of self-pity. Let her scream and shout and accuse me of being selfish. I didn't care; I knew exactly what she was doing anyway. Really, deep down, she felt bad about not picking Lacey up herself; after all, it wasn't like she'd been at work all day or anything, she'd just been 'out.'

But that was too hard for her to admit to herself, see; it was easier for her to blame me. That way she could keep on believing she was a good mom and if only she didn't have such a lazy, good-for-nothing son, everything would be all right.

After a few minutes I could feel her looking at me, and I glanced round a bit to see how she was looking at me. Her eyes were dry by then, but the expression on her face was cold and hard and bitter.

Some people said I'd got eyes like my mom, but I didn't think so. A girl once told me I'd got puppy-dog eyes. I'm not really sure what 'puppy-dog eyes' are like, but I was certain at that minute that my mom didn't have them. She had a full-grown, fighting Pit Bull's eyes maybe, but they're not the same, are they?

She kept that look up for what seemed like ages. Then she shook her head again, took a long drag on the cigarette and sighed loudly. She picked up her bag and got her mobile phone out to ring the school. We hadn't had a proper phone for years; it'd been cut-off when my mom didn't pay the bill. But luckily she had some credit on her mobile, and even more luckily, Lacey was still at the school and was OK.

'No thanks to you, you useless little git.' These were my mom's last words as she stormed out of the house and slammed the front door behind her.

I sat there for a while gazing at the T.V. Now I had a choice: I could either sit there and feel bad until my mom got home with Lacey, and then try and make things OK again, or, I could get changed, take the lager from the fridge and go round to Chris's party.

'Slag,' I shouted out loud, as I stood up and ran up the stairs two at a time. I deliberately left my dirty plate on the living room floor for Tyson to lick clean. I had a shower and found something to wear. The jeans weren't exactly sparkling and the T-shirt could've done with an iron, but it would be dark at the party, and the creases would drop out eventually. I threw my school uniform in the corner and promised myself I'd remember to wash and iron it ready for Monday morning.

Downstairs, I decided I'd just take four of the cans of lager. My mom was already in a bad mood, and if she came home to find the fridge emptied of alcohol, then she'd take it out on Lacey. I gave Tyson a bit of a pat and a stroke, then picked up the cans, left the house and walked round to my mate's.

Chris's sister, Gemma, opened the door. 'Hey-up, gorgeous,' she laughed, and she gave me a big hug.

The house was warm. There was a sweet smell in the air and I smiled. I left my cans of lager on the table in the kitchen and chose a bottle of Stella instead; that was a lot stronger than the cheap stuff my mother bought. Then I walked into the living room and claimed a spot on the settee. It was comfortable and nice, and after cadging a cigarette from a dopey but keen looking girl, I reckoned I was set up for the night.

I was still a bit uptight inside; I pictured that look on my mother's face and I shivered. But I was glad I'd come to the party and I was looking forward to having a good time.

As it got later, the music got louder, the house got fuller, and I got more and more drunk. There were loads of kids who I knew off the estate there and I really began to lighten up. The rough day I'd had began to fade from my mind and I laughed, drank and smoked along with everybody else.

And then, about midnight, I saw Mel – that lass from school. I wasn't sure if she'd been there all night, but if she had, I was surprised I hadn't noticed her earlier. She was talking to Gemma and giggling – and she looked hot.

She sort of stood out, you know? She was so confident and you could tell she just loved herself. She was different to the girls who I usually went with. Her clothes were better, her hair was shinier, and her make-up didn't look like it'd been put on with a paintball gun. She was quieter and she didn't swear in every sentence. But there was one thing I couldn't help noticing was the same; she was just as tough.

Mel laughed again more loudly than before, and as she flicked her long dark hair away from her face, she caught my eye, and she looked at me for a few seconds longer than she needed to. The group of lads who I was sitting with began to follow my gaze, and when they saw who I was looking at, the crude comments and laughter that went with any conversation about a fit looking bird began.

Slang

I told them I knew her and that she'd be no problem.

Chris laughed. 'In your dreams, lover boy. She wouldn't look at you twice, you scrubber.'

I laughed back, it wasn't disrespectful for us to call each other 'scrubber;' we knew it was just a joke. But if the other kids called us anything like that, it would usually cause a fight.

'No problem,' I repeated. 'Just you watch.'

And with that, I wandered over to Mel and began to talk.

A lot of the time I'm not much of a talker. Firstly, I think it's because everybody's always talking at me: my mother, the teachers, Lacey. Basically I didn't have to talk; they all managed to keep the 'conversation' running along just fine by themselves. Secondly, with the girls who I usually spent my time with, I didn't need to say an awful lot. They were happy enough without the speeches; it wasn't my words they were after.

But Mel wasn't going to be like that, she was going to make me work. She was so cool. She put a blank look on her face, stared straight into my eyes and waited to see what I could possibly do to impress her.

This was new to me and I found it different; interesting. challenge

'Didn't expect to see you here,' I said, and I smiled one of my most charming smiles. 'Glad I have though.'

She didn't reply, but there was a hesitation. It wasn't a brush off; a girl with her confidence would've told me to get lost straight away if that'd been what she meant. But Mel didn't; she just kept on staring. Something was still holding her back a bit, but she was interested all right.

I kept smiling and half wondered if she was pleased by what I'd said; whether she'd been secretly watching me during all those boring maths lessons? Or, perhaps she was just after a good time and anybody would do? Maybe she'd had a row with her parents that night as well, and this was her way of getting back at them; knowing how gutted they'd be if they discovered their little girl was getting smashed at a sleazy party on a rough estate and being hit on by a kid they'd hate.

I soon stopped wondering though, and went back to sweet-talking Mel. I didn't care what her reasons were anyway; the point was, I was here and she was here and the lads over in the corner were waiting.

'You look really nice,' I went on, and I reached out my hand and ran it softly down her arm. 'I've never seen you out of school uniform before, you look great.'

For a split second and without really wanting to, Mel smiled. It was a smug smile, but it was definitely a smile. She tried to cover it up quick though, by having a right long drink from the bottle she was holding.

I watched her carefully and tried to work out exactly how drunk she was. It wasn't easy. Her eyes were just starting to mist over a bit, but she still seemed steady enough and in control. I decided that she'd probably smiled because she was flattered, rather than because she was out of it; I was doing well.

'You look old,' she said out of nowhere. 'You look too old to be still going to school.'

She was right I suppose, as I stood there with a bottle in one hand and a cigarette in the other, I was hardly the image of typical school boy; but then again, I don't think I ever had been.

'Well, I won't be going for much longer will I? A few more months and I'll be free.'

'Like you'll notice the difference,' she said smartly. 'You're hardly a regular attender as it is.'

I smiled at the dig. She still couldn't quite let herself be nice to me. 'What are you going to do when you leave?' I asked her, like I genuinely cared and was interested.

'I'm going to study medicine,' Mel announced, and she said it in the tone of voice that most people would've used to tell you that Tuesdays follow Mondays.

For some reason, it made me want to laugh. I mean you could just imagine it if she ever took me home to tea, couldn't you?

'Hi, darling, who's this you've brought home?'

'Mummy, Daddy; this is my new boyfriend, Danny.'

'Hello there, young Daniel, and where do you live?'

'Oh I live on the biggest estate in Sheffield. You know, the one with all the burned out cars, boarded up buildings, gangs, graffiti, crack houses ...'

'How lovely. And what would you like to do when you leave school?'

'Ah well, I've got lots of opportunities open to me. I've received training in petty crime, cannabis farming and benefit fraud.'

'Well, that's super. I'm sure you will both be very happy together. Now, would you like caviar or lobster for starters?'

Yeah, right!

Anyway, me and Mel carried on talking for a bit longer. I asked her how she'd ended up at the party and she told me, but I wasn't really listening. I used the time to move a little closer, get my arm around her shoulder and make the most of my puppy-dog eyes.

A few cracks began to appear in the hard front that she'd put on, and she soon started to soften up.

She even laughed when I said the only reason Chris had such a big telly, was because he was trying to make up for other things in his life that were so tiny.

I can't say she was exactly throwing herself at me, but she never once pulled away or looked anything but pleased – or smug maybe – but she definitely didn't try to put me off.

Within twenty minutes we were going upstairs together. I guided her across the living room with my hand on her back, and as we passed the group of lads, I smirked at Chris and winked.

THREE

I probably hadn't been on my best form that night due to all the Stella. But Mel had seemed happy enough, and after we'd done I even offered to walk her home.

She said she was sleeping over at a mate's though, and she went. I snuggled back down into the warm bed and closed my eyes; I ended up staying at Chris's all night.

About a week later I decided to show my face at school again, and we were outside our form room when I saw Mel. I hadn't really known how to be with her at first – this 'posh' girl thing was all new to me. But she behaved just like she always had done; she didn't go out of her way to speak to me and she didn't avoid me either.

For a bit, I even wondered if she actually remembered what'd happened; I mean I'd sort of expected some reaction. But there was nothing, and that was fine with me. I was relieved she didn't start hanging around wanting to see me again, and I was also glad she didn't get the face on and start acting like she was disgusted or like I'd taken advantage.

analyse

A few weeks went by and I didn't give it anymore thought. Then, one Monday morning, the alarm clock woke me up as usual. I shivered, and as I leaned over to turn the alarm off, I noticed that there was ice on the inside of my bedroom window. I pulled up the blankets and decided to give school a miss – again.

But unfortunately, Lacey had other ideas. A couple of minutes later she came running into my bedroom shouting, 'Come on, Danny, get up. I've got to get ready. We're practicing for the school play today so I've got to go; I'm the star. Come on, come on. Please take me to school.'

She was shaking my shoulder as hard as she could and jumping up and down. I opened my eyes and looked at her.

'Pleeease,' she said again, and she put her head on one side, grinned a toothless grin and tried to wink.

I thought about it. I was right comfy in bed and I really didn't want to get up, but she was still grinning and her eyes were big and sort of sparkly. I didn't want to make them cry, so I gave in.

'OK then, I'll take you. But you need to get ready – now,' I said.

'Yes!' she screeched loudly, and she went skipping off back into her bedroom.

Just as we were leaving the house half an hour later, a taxi pulled up and my mom got out. She'd not been home all night – which was particularly useless, even for her. She looked worse for wear, and she was swaying about as she paid the driver.

As we passed, she managed to give Lacey a kiss and say, 'Have a nice day, love, and be a good girl.'

Then she zigzagged up the path, concentrated hard to get her key in the lock and disappeared inside.

So much for parental guidance, eh?

When I eventually got to school, I found out that the mock exams were starting. Bleeding hell, I thought; I knew I'd have been better off staying in bed. But as it was, I sort of got swept along with everybody else towards the gym, and then we had to line up in alphabetical order. The corridor was really packed, but I noticed a couple of Mel's friends standing behind me and I could hear them whispering.

'That's him,' said one of them.

'No!' gasped the other.

I turned round a bit so I could just see them out of the corner of my eye. One was a real darling: she had long blonde hair and a right body on her. The other wasn't. She was a bit like Shrek, but uglier. I shuddered; you would've had to have had a few to even think about tackling her.

I looked down then, as though I hadn't heard them, and the fit one started whispering again. 'She said it happened at some party. Can you imagine it? I mean I know he's good looking, but ...'

'I know,' nodded Princess Fiona's grandma. 'Just look at the state of his clothes. And he's a right retard as well. He's always getting into trouble and having a go at someone. I just can't believe Mel did it.'

'Well, I bet she's regretting it now,' said the blonde one.

I snapped my head up and stared at them. Who the hell did they think they were?

They looked away quick, and seemed a bit scared. They probably thought I was going to pull a knife on them, or try to sell them weed, or have a go at seducing them, right there in the main corridor. Stupid bitches.

What kind of kid did they think I was? And what had it got to do with them anyway, what'd happened or how Mel felt about it?

We were called into the exam then, and I was glad to get away.

The gym had been set up with hundreds of single desks set out in perfect rows; each one had a grey plastic chair behind it. I sat down at the right one and nearly died when the teacher said we'd got two hours to complete the paper. What was I going to do for two hours?

I glanced up and decided to count the ceiling tiles; there were eight hundred and sixteen, I think. But that hadn't taken long and I soon started to get bored.

I stared at the exam paper. It reminded me of the last time I'd sat at a desk in the gym, which had been at the end of Year 9.

My attendance had been really bad that year. My mom had been with a bloke called Mick and they went out all the time. It was before Lacey had been old enough to go to school, and so I'd stayed at home a lot to look after her while my mom either wasn't there, or was in bed. During the first eight months of that year, my attendance had been fifteen percent.

That was the first time the Education Welfare people got really serious, and my mom got a summons. It sort of shook her up a bit. She didn't like the court thing at all, and on top of that, Mick wasn't keen on people turning up at the house and sticking their noses into what was happening. He soon got fed up and moved on, so my mom started staying in and looking after Lacey herself.

Anyway, when we got the exam results, it turned out I'd done OK. Not spectacular, but average, and to say that my attendance had been as bad as it had, and that I'd done an awful lot of staring out of windows and flicking rubbers about even when I was there, average was quite impressive. Maybe I was lucky, maybe I was a genius, who knows?

I looked down at the maths paper that was in front of me again. I flicked through and thought about having a go at some of the questions. But I just couldn't be arsed. I passed the rest of the time by staring at Mel's ugly friend and freaking her out.

At dinnertime, when the exam had finished, I went across to the shops to get something to eat and met up with Chris.

'We've just got Street Speed 4,' he grinned. 'It's right good. You wanna come round and have a go?'

Was there any decision to be made? The latest breakthrough in gaming technology, or mock GCSE science? Obviously not.

In the end, I missed all of the other mock exams that week as well. I just couldn't face them; school was bad enough on a good day, but when you had to sit there in silence and go for hours on end without a fag, it was just plain impossible.

***

It was one night a bit after that when two other things happened: one, Chris told me about their Lee, and two, I got arrested again.

We'd been hanging around on the estate and we'd been drinking, but we weren't drunk. It was freezing cold, and I'd wanted to go home, even though it was still only ten o'clock. But Chris had looked miserable when I'd suggested it.

'You do what you want,' he said. 'I'm gonna to stay out here.'

He looked like he had something on his mind, and knowing how he felt, I decided I'd keep him company for a bit longer.

After a couple of minutes it began to rain, and the rain soon turned to sleet. I pulled my hat down and the collar of my jacket up, but I could still feel the freezing sting as the drops of sleet ran down between my shoulder blades.

'Let's go in there.' Chris nodded towards one of the boarded up houses, and we ran up the path and round the back.

The shutters that the coun[?]
to the windows were un-mo[?]
back door had started to [?]
after a few hard kicks, it ga[?]
and Chris were in. We could ha[?]
thing. The odd street light that still work[?]
at least meant there was some light outside, but inside the house it was proper black. It was also right quiet; the only noise came from outside where a dog was barking its head off in one of the nearby gardens.

We stumbled through what must've been the kitchen and came to a room that still had carpet on the floor. Our eyes were getting used to the dark by then, and we could just about make out that there was no furniture in the room, so we both sat down on the floor and leaned back against the wall.

I'd got some bud that I'd bought earlier and was going to save, but I changed my mind and we shared some.

After a few minutes, Chris said, 'How's things at your house?'

'Usual,' I answered. I was surprised by the question, but I went on. 'My mom's got another new bloke. I haven't seen him yet – she hasn't even told me about him – I can just tell because she does herself up like a Christmas tree when she goes out, she puts s of perfume on ...' I paused. 'What ut you?'

We never usually talked about this kind of stuff, it was usually who'd banged who, or who'd scored with who, or who'd got locked up and what for, but I thought that tonight Chris needed to talk, and I was right.

After a deep sigh, he said, 'Our Lee's getting out tomorrow.'

Christ. I pulled a face like somebody'd just punched me.

'He's been let out early on a tag,' Chris carried on quietly. 'My mom said he couldn't come back to live with us at first, but he needed a proper address to be released to, and nobody else would have him. So she gave in and said he could come back home.'

I shook my head. Lee was Chris's older brother, and he was a complete nutcase. He'd been in loads of trouble a couple of years ago; the usual stuff at first: TWOCing, assaults, a bit of dealing; that sort of stuff. Stuff you just get supervision orders and reparation for, but then he'd stabbed a kid and that did it.

He got sent to what's know around here as 'Ilkatraz' – a prison not far away. I think it should've been for about four years, but

alkatraz

38

obviously he'd behaved himself and he was getting out early.

Chris took a long drag. 'I know I'm no angel, Danny, but you know what he's like; he's dangerous. He's gonna end up killing somebody. You remember that time with our Gemma?'

I hadn't remembered until then, but as soon as he said it I tensed up. Lee had hit Gemma once, only once, but hard enough to knock her out completely. She'd been playing some music one morning, Lee hadn't been in long and was still under the influence of something, I'm not sure what, but he'd hit her when she wouldn't turn it down. She ended up in the hospital for a whole week.

Lacey was annoying sometimes – a lot of the time in fact – but I'd never hit her. Lately, I'd even started sticking up for her when my mom did. It was ages since my mom or any of her blokes had hit me, but Lacey still got 'smacked' a lot. I didn't like it; she was only a little kid.

I have to admit though, I wasn't looking forward to having Lee back with us. I could see why Chris was so gutted; he actually had to live with him.

'Perhaps he won't come home,' I said, trying to be cheerful. 'It might be too dodgy. I mean, he upset a lot of people before he got banged up; maybe it'll be too risky for him to live back here?'

'Maybe,' Chris didn't sound convinced. 'It's just ...'

But I never found out what it just was, because at that minute a torch was shone in our eyes, and a voice shouted, 'Police. Lay down, lads; arms out to the side.'

Oh, for God's sake. Where had they come from?

I blinked as the light nearly blinded me.

'Down. Now!' One of them shouted again.

Me and Chris glanced at each other. What else could we do? I rolled over on to my side, and tried as hard as I could to lay down without actually letting my face touch that filthy carpet.

I know it might all seem a bit dramatic; cops, shouting, getting searched, but they always went over the top on our estate. Somebody must've tipped them off about us kicking the backdoor in, and obviously they'd got nothing better to do than come after us.

I could sort of see why they had to be careful; I mean, they didn't know what we were doing or taking, did they? But even so, there really wasn't any need for all that.

And it wasn't as if we were robbing some old coffin dodger of their life savings; the house wasn't even lived in. What damage could we really have done to a damp, stinking old dump that was totally empty and that even the rats wouldn't be seen dead in? We were hardly Britain's most wanted

For God's sake, I took a breath in and almost threw up from the stench, how unlucky were we?

I was fed up. I was tired. I was freezing cold. I could really have done without it. But, I told myself, we hadn't really done anything wrong. Maybe nothing would come of it; just a lecture, and then I'd be able to go home and go to bed. But of course, I was being way too optimistic.

The two coppers moved in slowly and began to search us. One was quite young and he started on Chris. The other was a right old git, and when he searched me he was a lot rougher than he needed to be. He prodded and pushed me around all over the place, and within a few seconds he found what was left of the bud. He stared at it for a while and I could tell he was wondering what to do. Was it worth the paperwork?

We could still get away with a shouting at, I hoped. But no ... at that very minute, the other one, the young one, produced some pills and a package from Chris's inside pocket. My heart dropped into my toes. I could've killed him. That was it; now there was no chance of an early night.

Before we knew it, we were sitting in the back of a cop car.

***

When we got to the police station, they put us in the cells while they tried to find an 'appropriate adult' to be with us. Not easy in our case. To be honest, I was surprised they found my mom at all. She'd sold the mobile phone, and so they said they'd go round to the house and fetch her when they got time. I was sure she wouldn't be there, but she was.

They took me to one of the interview rooms and when my mom walked in, I could tell she was mad. She gave me a quick, cold stare, then ignored me. She started talking to the copper in a fake voice.

'I'm really sorry he's causing you all this trouble,' she whined. 'I don't know where he gets it from.' She looked sad and shook her head.

This was a change to the usual script; usually she knew exactly where I got it from – my dad.

'I try my best,' she went on. 'But he just doesn't seem to care about anything I say or do; I can't do a thing with him.'

'Right,' said the copper, yawning. 'Shall we get on with it?'

He started going on about 'criminal damage' and 'breaking and entering' and 'possession,' even 'intent to supply' – but that was just to try and scare me, I had nowhere near enough bud on me for that and it wasn't wrapped.

All of my other orders with Youth Offending had finished, and so in the end nothing happened except a caution for possession; which was pointless really, and had just wasted six hours of everybody's time.

As we left, Chris's mom was still sitting in the waiting room. It looked like Chris was in for a long night. His mom and my mom passed a few minutes slagging us off, and wondering where we got it from and what else they could possibly have done to have made us into good lads.

How about staying in more, staying sober more and not shacking up with losers? I thought to myself; that would be a start. But I didn't say anything; I kept my head down. There'd be enough arguing and shouting when I got home, no need to start it off any earlier.

The buses had stopped running hours ago, and my mom said she'd no money for a taxi, so we got a lift home in a police car. As we drove along nobody spoke, but I could feel my mom getting more and more wound up. She lit a fag, but the driver told her to put it out. I decided I'd make a run for it, straight upstairs as soon as we got home. I wasn't scared of my mom anymore, but like I said, I was really tired and if I could avoid all the effort of shouting, I would.

But she started before we'd even walked in through the front door.

'I've just about had enough of you, you little sod. Are you really so thick you can't manage to keep yourself out of trouble?'

I ignored her and started to go upstairs, but that didn't put her off. We had no carpet on our stairs, and I could hear her heels thud on the bare floorboards as she came up after me.

'Are you fuckin' listening to me?' she screamed. 'I'm sick and tired of it. Bleedin' police knocking on my door all the time; me having to drop everything. For God's sake, I've got a life as well you know? But you just have to go and spoil everything for me, don't you? I hate you! We were having a nice night in ...'

She shut up.

I was about halfway up the stairs by then, but I stopped and turned round. She'd slipped up with the last bit, and she was trying to bluff her way out of it. She had a tough glare on her face that backed up everything she'd just said. She really did hate me.

I'd seen that look before, and heard most of the words before – a million times in fact, and on the whole I'd learned to live with it. But that night it hit a nerve. Maybe because I was so tired, maybe because she so obviously wanted to be with her new bloke, rather than with me – her son; maybe because ... oh I don't know why. But I totally lost it, and the fact that she'd shut up gave me a chance to have a go back, and I did.

'Oh here we go again,' I yelled in her face. 'Which hard-up bastard have you been throwing yourself at this time, eh? There's no wonder my dad left, and Lacey's dad left, and everybody else always leaves in the end, because you're just a dirty little slag and everybody knows it. For fuck's sake, you'd go with Jack the Ripper if he bought you half a lager. I wish you'd spend as much time with me and Lacey as you do with the tossers you're always shagging. I wish you cared about us as much.'

I was just getting warmed up now, and I had loads more to say. But as I stopped to take in some air, I heard a cry behind me.

I turned around and saw Lacey standing on the landing. She was only wearing a T-shirt, and she was shivering. Huge tears were running down her cheeks and she was trying to speak, but she couldn't. I looked back at my mom, and this time she didn't give me any cold or bitter or disgusted looks. This time, she couldn't look at me – or Lacey – at all.

She turned away and went back downstairs.

Slowly, I went up to where Lacey was standing. 'Go back to bed,' I said, trying to be gentle. 'It's alright, don't cry. Go on; you'll freeze to death.'

Lacey hesitated, then she threw her arms around my middle and buried her head in my jacket. I didn't know what to do; I wasn't used to hugs – not from family, anyway. But after a second, I lifted up my hand and stroked the top of her head. Her hair was really soft; sort of fluffy.

'Go on,' I said again, but she still didn't move. So I picked her up, carried her back into her bedroom and put her into bed.

She clung to me for ages then, and when she'd finally stopped crying and I'd wiped her eyes with the sleeve of my jacket, she whispered, 'Are you going to go away?'

'No, don't be daft. It was just a row, that's all; we'll get over it.' My cheerful voice was obviously false. But she didn't say anything else; she just gripped my jacket hard, and kept on looking at me. Maybe her eyes were like a puppy-dog's eyes, I thought to myself.

When Lacey eventually dropped back off to sleep, I went into my bedroom and flopped down on the bed.

I felt in my pockets for the bud, then remembered the cops still had it. I did find a cigarette though, and as I smoked it, I began to think about the shit night I'd had.

So that's why my mom had been in the house tonight I thought; she'd had her new bloke round. Oh well, at least letting it slip out had stopped her screaming at me anymore. She always acted odd when she told me about a new boyfriend – I don't know why, you'd think she'd be used to it by now. I wondered who this one was, what he'd be like and when he'd be moving in.

Not that it was usually that bad for me now though. I was older and I'd seen it all before; I just stayed out more once they started hanging around the house.

But Lacey was still little, and she'd sometimes get upset when somebody new was on the scene. Usually, she was just forgotten about for a while, but sometimes I got the feeling she was actually scared of them, and I didn't like that.

I laid and thought about things for a bit longer, and although I was still wound up, the cigarette calmed me down enough to let me sleep.

I didn't get up for school the next morning, which meant that Lacey didn't either. My mom gave me the silent treatment for about a week, and the atmosphere in the house was colder than ever.

But then it was Christmas and my mom cheered right up. She got some flashy jewellery from her new boyfriend and she was well pleased. Surprise surprise, I didn't hear anything from my dad – he didn't even manage a card. But my mom gave me a wad of money that she'd got from somewhere, and Lacey's present was this doll thing that cried and peed and stuff, so she was dead chuffed.

The Christmas dinner came out of packets, but hey, waiting for the microwave to go ping was the nearest my mom ever got to cooking, so really, that was her putting in effort.

We had a few drinks and we had a few laughs, and we ended up having an OK Christmas.

The New Year though, was to be a very different story.

FOUR

It was New Year's Eve and me and Chris were going out. I went round to his house early and he wasn't quite ready, so once he'd let me in, he disappeared back upstairs. I would've normally walked straight into the living room, but that night Lee was there, laid on the settee watching a DVD.

I could see him from where I was standing in the kitchen, and I decided to stay where I was. I didn't really know what to say to him or how to act around him. One minute he was your best buddy, the next he was threatening to rip your head off.

Anyway, as I was standing there, Gemma came in through the back door.

'Hi, Danny,' she said. Then she looked at me a bit strange and added, 'You talked to Mel lately?'

This came totally out of the blue; nobody had mentioned Mel to me for ages. Chris had asked of course, the day after the party, but that was all.

'Haven't talked to her for weeks,' I said. 'Why?'

Gemma looked past me and out of the window as she spoke. 'It's just ... well, she might want to talk to you, that's all.'

I didn't have a clue what she was on about. I thought it must've been something bad though, because of the way she was acting.

When Gemma looked at me again, she could see that I hadn't got it, and she smiled like she felt sorry for me; like I was a little kid who needed things spelling out for him.

'It's probably nothing,' she said, shaking her head a bit and smiling again. But the smile wasn't real.

Just then, Lee came into the kitchen. He'd grown upwards and outwards since he'd been inside – due to the three square meals a day I suppose. He stood in front of me and nodded downwards. I looked behind and realised I was standing in front of the fridge.

'Oh, sorry, mate,' I said, and I shifted out of the way quick.

He didn't answer. He just got a can of Coke out and went back into the living room. Which was good.

I would've asked Gemma more about Mel then, but she'd gone; she must've slipped out when Lee came in. I thought about what she'd said again, and I'd just decided that I'd try and see Mel and find out what was up, when I heard Chris's footsteps thudding down the stairs.

'Come on then, Danny boy; let's be off. I don't think we're going to have the time of our lives standing in our kitchen!' Chris was buzzin'. 'I've had a bit of luck today,' he added in a quieter voice, and he slid some notes out of his back pocket, just enough for me to see the tops. 'Come on, let's treat ourselves.'

Chris grinned, and I grinned back, and ... I completely forgot about Mel the minute we walked out of Chris's back door.

We did treat ourselves that night. I mean even for us, we really tret ourselves.

We went into town to a club. The tickets had been quite expensive at one time, but Lee had 'acquired' them from somewhere and he'd let us and a couple of other kids off the estate have them cheap.

Usually, me and Chris didn't have much trouble getting into clubs, even though we weren't really old enough. But with it being New Year's Eve and all, we thought we'd be extra careful; they might be a bit more picky than normal. We'd sorted out some fake I.D. and we knew it'd be a good idea to join up with some girls; mixed groups always got in easier than just lads on their own. So we scanned the long row of people and we both noticed a couple of decent looking girls near the front.

'They'll do,' Chris said, and he started to walk over to them. I followed, but I kept my distance a bit.

'Excuse me,' Chris said in a fake posh voice. 'Have either of you got a light?'

They looked at him for about a second, shook their heads and then ignored him. I smiled at his sad attempt, and when he looked round and saw me, he smiled as well, and then he mouthed, 'piss-off'.

He turned back and had another go. 'I think you go to the same college as me; Shirecross? Is that right?'

This, of course, was a complete lie – but it was also a good guess.

'Yes, we do,' said the girl who was nearest to him. 'I don't recognise you though, what are you studying?'

'Psychology and Sport and Leisure,' Chris replied.

I just couldn't keep a straight face, and I had to turn away quick. As far as Chris knew, psychology started with an 's', and his idea of 'Sport and Leisure' was getting shagged one night then having a lay-in the next morning.

I don't think the lasses really believed him either, but they were being nice and they said, 'Oh' and nodded.

Chris took his chance and carried on. 'I'm Christopher, and this is Daniel,' he said, as he got hold of my jacket and pulled me over to them. 'I know you'll recognise Daniel; every girl who's ever seen him remembers him.'

I gave him a filthy look, but he didn't see me. He was grinning at the girls, and they, still being polite, were smiling back.

Chris went on a real roll then; making up all sorts of shit about himself and me. It made me cringe.

As the queue moved forward, Chris and the girls all talked away at each other. But it was soon obvious that talking to us would be as far as they'd go. So once we'd got past the doormen, we mingled in with the crowd and lost them.

The club was wicked. It was always a good night out, but I suppose the special occasion had given everybody an extra buzz. The music blasted away and the place was packed. I remember laughing a lot that night, at least at the beginning.

I have to admit though, the laughing was helped along a lot by what we'd had.

We'd bought it inside the club from a dealer off our estate called Karl.

Karl was a right nasty piece of work. He was about forty-five, as wide as a door and rock hard. He always wore loads of chunky gold chains and rings and stuff, and to be honest, he looked stupid – but did anybody ever tell him that? No, cos they'd have been bonkers to.

A lot of people had been hurt bad by Karl, and normally, just being within a mile of him would've made me feel on edge. But everything seemed so relaxed and happy that night, that I thought it'd probably be OK. I gave Chris some money and let him sort it out.

A bit later, I was staring at this girl on the dance floor. She had this bright green dress on, and it was only just long enough to cover her back-side. She was laughing and singing along to all the tunes, and I could hardly take my eyes off her. Then I heard Chris's voice behind me.

'Look,' he said.

I followed his eyes and saw their Lee walking towards us through the crowd. He had a huge smirk on his ugly face.

'How's he managed that?' I shouted over the music. I meant with him being tagged and having a seven 'til seven curfew.

'He'll have taken it off and left it at home – he's done it before,' Chris shouted back.

Lee came over and started talking to Chris. I couldn't hear what about, but I wasn't too worried because he was still smiling. I decided to leave them to it, and I went over to the girl.

She was called Roxi and she was a right laugh. She giggled at everything I said, and she chatted away as though we'd known each other for ten years rather than ten minutes. She wasn't shy either. When she kissed me she really meant it, and her hands were all over the place.

I was just about to ask her if she wanted to go somewhere else, when there was a huge crash from near the bar. It must have been loud, because everybody heard it above the music and turned round to see what was happening.

Two blokes were standing amongst a load of broken glass shouting at each other. I couldn't tell what they were saying because the music was still banging away, but I could see that they meant business. I recognised the one who was standing furthest away as Karl. His eyes were blinking madly as he waved his arms about and then pointed and snarled at the other bloke. The other one had his back to me at first, but as he bent down to pick up a broken glass, he turned to one side slightly and I saw his face – it was Lee. You remember I told you about Lee's temper? Well he was a right pussy compared to Karl.

This was going to be one big bust up. Karl would have friends there, Lee would have friends there, and I knew from experience how easy it was to get dragged into a scrap like this. I decided that I'd rather not get cut to shreds so early in the New Year, and I'd just got hold of Roxi's hand to lead her away, when I felt a tug on my sleeve.

It was Chris. He didn't say anything, but the look on his face said, 'He is my brother.'

I looked back at my new found friend and sighed. Oh well darling, maybe another time, I thought. I squeezed her hand and said, 'I've got to go.'

She started to say something, but I don't know what, because I turned to Chris again and nodded. You can't just run out on a mate, can you? loyalty

The bouncers had bulldozed through the crowd and I lost sight of Lee and Karl for a few seconds. When I saw them again, Lee's face was covered in blood and Karl was being pulled off him by a couple of the bouncers. As I'd expected, loads of other fights were beginning to break out and a lot of people were leaving quickly.

Karl was going absolutely crazy to get free; he was kicking out and pulling and twisting in all directions. The two bouncers were struggling to keep hold, and when he made a big push forward, all three of them ended up on the floor and one had to let go. The other two, who'd been holding Lee, went over to help and although me and Chris were both worse for wear, we knew this would be our only chance. Somehow, we managed to grab Lee and drag him out of the club.

I'm pretty sure the security guys didn't see us, but as Karl screamed and shouted about what he was going to do to Lee, he was looking straight at us.

We were all in a bad way – especially Lee – but we had to walk all the way home from town and it was hard. A couple of times, Lee passed out on his feet and we had to hold him up.

But once, he got all worked up and started going on about Karl. In between all the threats and swearing, he also let it slip what the row had been about. It seemed that Lee had been doing his own bit of business in the club that night, which had obviously pissed Karl right off. Me and Chris looked at each other and I shook my head. What was he playing at? He must have been mad to deal anywhere near Karl; he was lucky to still be breathing. ✳ drug-war (rivalry)

Eventually, we got to Chris's house and dumped Lee on the settee. He looked like he was going to go to sleep at first, but then suddenly, his eyes flipped wide open and he went completely crazy again. It was definitely time to go.

I stumbled in through our front door and saw that my mom had passed out on the settee. I half wondered why she wasn't out with her new bloke, but everything was whizzing around too much for me to wonder about it for long. I left her where she was and went into the kitchen. I was starving, but as usual, the cupboards were bare; so I went up to bed – even though I knew I wouldn't be able to sleep for hours. ✳

***

The next day I got woken up by Lacey's new doll thing crying on the landing. For God's sake; I thought the batteries would've run out by now, but oh no, it bawled and it bawled and it bawled. I forced my eyes open and saw that it was three o'clock in the afternoon. My head was heavy and my eyes were stinging.

I tried to sit up a bit, but the second my head left the pillow I felt sick; I mean really, really sick. I hadn't had anything to eat since my dinner the day before, which was lucky really, because I'm sure if there'd been anything inside me I'd have thrown up all over the bed. But as it was, I just retched. I felt a burning in my throat as some hot, bitter tasting stuff came up from my stomach. Not knowing what else to do, I swallowed it again – it tasted foul.

Carefully, I put my head back down on to the pillow, took a deep breath and tried to get back to sleep. But the screaming doll on the landing was really getting to me by then.

'Lacey, shut that bloody doll up!' I yelled.

But she wasn't there, and it carried on. I put the pillow over my head and ears and pressed it down hard; that was a bit better at least.

I must have dropped off eventually, even though the racket carried on, and the next time I woke up, it was dark outside again.

I sat up slowly and put my feet to the floor. After a few seconds I stood upright, steadying myself with one hand on the bed. I'd never felt that rough after a night out before, and it made me think that what we'd bought wasn't exactly what it should've been. But I suppose that's the chance you take, isn't it?

I was still a bit wobbly, but I set off downstairs, hoping that something to eat and drink would sort me out.

As I eased myself down one step at a time, I started to hear voices in the kitchen. One was my mom, the other was a bloke. I stopped and tried to listen.

'So I'll bring my stuff round tomorrow then, sweetheart,' he said.

'I can't wait,' my mom giggled.

I heard footsteps as they came out of the kitchen and in a better state of health I would've made it back upstairs in time, but before I'd even turned round, they'd come into the hall and seen me.

And I could not believe my eyes. I just froze. Standing there, in our hall, was Karl.

'Oh, this is our Danny,' my mom said, looking in my direction. 'Lazy little bugger's only just got out of bed – you won't see much of him.'

'Alright?' Karl looked at me and nodded slightly as he spoke.

If he had recognised me, he wasn't letting on. I had no idea what to say to him, but it didn't matter. He'd already turned away and he was halfway out of the door before he remembered my mom.

'See you later, baby,' he said, and he leaned forward and kissed her.

Even after he'd gone, it was still a few seconds before I could actually speak. Then I managed, 'Mom, what the hell do you think you're doing?'

She looked at me blankly, and said, 'What do you mean?'

'*What do I mean?* I mean him; that dickhead. How can you even think about letting him move in? He's the biggest dealer around here. He's a complete psycho. He cuts people up.'

'Danny, that'll do. He's not a psycho at all; he's been really nice to me. And as for the biggest dealer around here, don't be so stupid. I know he dabbles a bit, but doesn't everybody?'

I couldn't believe what she was saying. What was up with her?

She was standing there gazing at the door, and it was clear that she was totally gone on him. I knew, deep down, there was no point trying anymore; I knew she wasn't going to change her mind. But I just couldn't stop myself. Without thinking about it, I got hold of her hand and spoke quietly.

'Please, Mom, I mean it, please don't let him come and live here. You must know what he's really like. Don't let him live here. Not with us; not with Lacey.'

She shook her hand out of mine. 'Oh, don't be daft, Danny. It'll all be OK; just you wait and see.'

She said this as though she was talking to a toddler who was crying because he'd grazed his knee. Then she went back into the kitchen, and I heard the sound of a ring-pull being opened.

I sat down on the stairs. She'd pulled some tossers in her time, my mom. Blokes who'd cheated on her, blokes who'd nicked off her, blokes who'd made her life – and our lives – miserable. But Karl? He was in a different league. He was going to be a bloody nightmare.

All I could think about for days after that was Karl. But then I went back to school, and all of a sudden, there was something else on my mind.

FIVE

'You'll be expecting a Fathers' Day card this year then, Danny?'

The comment came from a lad called Steve as we were waiting for the bus home from school. He was laughing and so were a few of the other kids round about. I frowned for a second, then gave him a tough stare. I'd never liked him; he always had a lot to say. 'Gob on legs' Chris called him.

I looked away then and reached into my pocket for a fag and a lighter. A million thoughts went in and out of my head. Was he just joking? Or did he really know something? If he did, then who? When? I couldn't sort it all out. But then he gave me my answer.

'Aah, won't it be sweet, you and Melanie and a bouncing bundle of joy ...'

I didn't hear the rest, because at that minute, I realised. I realised what he meant; what Gemma had meant a few days before.

'Shut the fuck up!' I shouted as I set off towards him.

His face froze and he backed off. Normally, I don't think he would've been that scared of me, but I suppose I reacted a lot worse than he expected. He'd obviously thought I already knew about Mel and he was just trying to wind me up a bit.

But my eyes must've been wild. I could feel my heart thudding in my chest and I wanted to kill him. I stepped forward another pace and pushed him hard. He fell back into the bus shelter and there was a thud as his head hit the glass. I watched him as he stumbled and tried to get his balance back. Then I threw my fag away, grabbed hold of his jacket with both hands and yanked his head up. 'I'll break your skull, you stupid little ...'

He was looking straight at me, and all at once, it hit me how panicky his eyes were. Then I noticed the colour had drained from his face and sweat was shining on his forehead. good decision

That was what stopped me I suppose. Seeing it made me think of something else for a second, and that gave me a chance to calm down. Not a lot, but enough to stop me wanting to murder him.

I could see then he hadn't really done that much wrong. It wasn't his fault I was the last to know. mature

But I was still mad.

'I'll kill you if you open your big gob again. You got that?' My voice was quiet, but I meant what I said and he knew it.

He nodded a bit, and as I let him go, I felt his shoulders drop.

Without looking at anybody else, I turned around and decided to walk home. I moved fast and my mind jumped about all over the place. I thought about the party, about going upstairs with Mel, about us ... 'sleeping' together. I thought about Gemma and what she'd said. How could I have forgotten?

Then I thought about Steve's words: 'Fathers' Day card.'

Father.

It couldn't be true. It just couldn't be. I mean, why? It'd never happened before, and with Mel it'd only been the once. You hear about people, don't you? People who try for years to have a kid; pay thousands of pounds to get themselves pregnant. So why should it happen to us?

I swore out loud and kicked an empty pop bottle that was lying on the floor. Then a new idea crossed my mind. For a few seconds, I felt better. Even if she was pregnant, and I still didn't know that for certain, it didn't mean it was definitely mine. I mean it could be anybody's; half the lad's in our bloody school.

But then I thought about her again and I wasn't so sure. To say she was usually so full of herself, and to say she'd had a fair bit to drink that night, maybe she had changed when we got upstairs. I didn't think about it at the time; I wouldn't have done, would I? But looking back now, maybe she had been a bit ... shy. Maybe she hadn't done it before.

Shit. So then, if it was mine, there was something else I didn't get; how come she hadn't told me? How come she'd carried on behaving exactly the same as she always had done? Not talking, not smiling; acting as though I was invisible. I knew she was stuck up and I knew I wasn't, but for God's sake, if she was going to have my kid you'd have thought she'd have let me in on the fact. The whole school seemed to know about it, so why didn't I?

There was only one way I was going to find out. I stopped in my tracks and changed direction, and instead of going home, I went to Chris's house.

Gemma looked surprised as she opened the back door. 'Chris's not in,' she said.

'No, it's you I want ... it's about Mel.'

'Oh right.' She stepped back and I followed her into the house.

I sat down and said, 'Is it true she's pregnant?'

Gemma shrugged a bit. 'That's what everybody's been saying, Danny. I honestly don't know, but I wouldn't be surprised; she's been off a few times lately and she never is usually. She keeps throwing up.'

I closed my eyes for a second, then said, 'Do you know where she lives?'

'Not exactly. But I know it's one of those new houses, and her second name's Carter – it might be in the phone book.'

Gemma got out the local phone directory and flicked through. 'Here it is,' she said. 'Ten, Milldale Close.'

'I might phone her instead,' I thought out loud. I wasn't exactly looking forward to that phone call, but it had to be better than turning up at her house and being met by her loving parents.

Gemma passed me the phone, 'Go on then; get it over with.'

I started to feel sick, and as she read out the number and I pressed the buttons on the phone, my hands were shaking like mad. nervous

It rang a couple of times, then a man's voice answered, 'Dr Carter speaking.'

turning point

68

I nearly slammed the phone straight back down then; maybe I should wait? But Gemma looked at me as though to say, 'Go on; you've got to.'

So I took a deep breath. 'Is Mel there please?' My voice sounded strange; partly because I was so shaky, and partly because I was trying to sound polite and not too rough.

'Who's calling?'

I'd hoped he wouldn't ask that. 'It's Danny, I … I know her from school.'

'Just a minute,' he said, and there was silence. I looked up at Gemma, but she was gazing in the opposite direction, trying hard to seem like she wasn't listening. After a few seconds I heard the phone being picked up again.

'Hello.' Mel's voice was quiet, but still confident.

'It's Danny.'

'Yes, I know.' She sounded sulky; like I was bugging her and she wished I'd leave her alone. That wound me up me a bit; I mean, I was trying my best here.

'I think I need to see you,' I said, being more stroppy than I meant to. 'Where can we meet?'

She was quiet for a long time, then she said, 'Outside Chubbies, tomorrow night.'

'No.' My voice was firm, 'It's got to be tonight.'

There was another pause, then obviously without wanting to, she said, 'OK, about seven.'

And that was it. I heard a click and a long beep; she'd put the phone down.

Gemma looked at me, and I told her what Mel had said – which didn't take long.

'Maybe she couldn't talk; perhaps there was somebody else there,' Gemma said.

I thought about it and hoped she was right; otherwise, this was going to be one hell of a difficult night.

***

When I got home my mom had made some tea. I won't say 'cooked' because as you know, she doesn't do cooking. She was making an effort to feed us though since Karl had moved in. It's part of the happy families game that we all have to play at the beginning.

It was Sod's Law I still felt too sickly to eat anything, though.

Karl was in the living room, talking quietly on his mobile phone. I'd been working hard at avoiding him, and so far I was doing fairly well. So like most days now, I went straight upstairs out of the way.

I laid on my bed and the time dragged. It was strange; I was dreading meeting Mel in a lot of ways, but on the other hand, I couldn't wait to get it over with. Things didn't usually get to me to like this. I mean normally, I could tell myself I didn't care about anything – I was good at it; I'd been doing it for a long time. But this was really doing my head in.

I thought about there being a baby that was mine. Baby. Every time I heard the word in my head it made me feel nervous.

Eventually it was time to get ready, and I tried to make myself look OK.

I was out of the house and halfway up the path when I heard my mom's voice behind me. 'Danny.'

'What?' I turned round to see her standing in the front doorway.

'Take our Lacey over to Aunty Sam's for me, will you?'

'I can't. I've got to go.'

'Oh go on, it won't take long.'

'Mom, I can't, I ...'

I shut up as Karl came and stood at my mom's side.

'*You*, are gonna do exactly what your mam tells you to,' he said slowly, and he lifted up his eyebrows. *threatning*

I looked away and swore silently. 'OK. Where is she?'

Even though I was really pissed off, I was careful not show any attitude; I knew it was best not to get too clever.

'That's a good lad,' Karl grinned as I walked back into the house, and he reached out and pressed his hand down hard on my shoulder. 'Son,' he added.

I glanced down at his hand, then up at his face. He was staring straight at me and it made me want to pull away. But he kept a tight grip on me, and there was nothing I could do but look down and wait.

When he did let me go, I turned to my mom. She was standing there with a soppy smile on her face that almost said 'Aah'. She really thought that what Karl had just done was some kind of an effort to bond with me. The stupid cow.

It would've bothered me a whole lot more if I hadn't been in such a rush, but as it was, all I could think about was getting out of the house.

It turned out that my mom had arranged for Lacey to sleep over at Sam's, so I had to wait for her to get her stuff together, then take her the ten minute walk in the opposite direction. Aunty Sam wasn't a real aunt – just somebody who my mom had known for a long time. She was OK though, and I felt happier leaving Lacey there than at home.

So that was one thing to be happy about, I suppose.

***

Chubbies was a fast food place in the middle of a row of shops across from our school. They did the most spectacular burgers there, with their own cheese and garlic sauce.

The off-license and all the take-aways were still open, and their lights lit up the pavement. *setting*

Loads of people were about but none of them was Mel. Of course, I was quite late by then, and I wondered if she'd been and gone already; somehow, I didn't think she'd have hung about for more than thirty seconds if she'd got there on time and I hadn't.

I stopped and waited.

Have you ever noticed how many babies there are about? No, I hadn't until then. But as I stood there watching, it seemed like every woman who passed was either pushing a pram or pregnant.

There was a newsagents next door, and I went in and bought some fags. After my third one, I asked a bloke what time it was, and he said it was five past eight. Well, she won't be coming now, I thought; either she'd not turned up at all, or I'd missed her.

I didn't know what to do. Obviously there was no point staying there any longer, but I really didn't want to go away and still not know what was happening. In my mind, I heard Gemma's voice reading out Mel's address. I suppose I had no other choice; if I wanted to get this sorted tonight, I'd have to go round to her house.

***

It took me about half an hour to walk to the new estate where she lived. It was only small though, and I found Milldale Close easily. It was a cu-de-sac of about twelve houses, and as I turned on to it, I stopped and looked at them. They were all big and detached, and each one had a clean, tidy garden in front of it. It seemed like there was a BMW or a four wheel drive parked on every driveway. Some of the houses still had their Christmas decorations up, and their porches glowed with different coloured lights. Everything was still and quiet.

I walked on until I saw which one was number ten. I was breathing hard and my mouth had gone dry.

I almost didn't do it. I almost turned around and ran. But then I did; I went up and I knocked on the front door.

A little dog started yapping its head off on the other side. Then a tall, grey haired bloke opened the door and I felt warm air on my face.

He looked me up and down and said, 'Yes?'

'I, err, just wondered if Mel's in,' I managed.

'Oh, right. Yes she is. I'll just call her for you.' He left the door open, went over to the bottom of the stairs and shouted, 'Melanie, there's someone here to see you.'

Mel was on her way down the stairs within a few seconds, but when she saw me in the doorway she stopped dead. She looked at me like I was a super-sized cockroach.

Then, with a big effort, she said, 'Wait there, I'll get my coat.'

'You don't have to go out,' her dad said, looking worried. 'He can come in if you want.'

'No!' Mel said, far too loudly. But then she calmed herself down a bit and added, 'It's OK, Dad, it's just about some homework; it'll only take a minute.'

We were halfway down the street and I'd had chance to light a fag before she spoke to me.

'What are you doing here?' she said through her teeth.

'I needed to see you. You weren't at Chubbies when I got there, so –'

'I was there at seven o'clock,' she snapped. 'When I was supposed to be!'

'Alright,' I said, 'It wasn't my fault, I had to –

'I don't care what you had to do; what do you want?'

This wasn't a good start. She was mad at me for standing her up at Chubbies, and she was mad at me for turning up at her house. This next bit was going to be a right laugh, wasn't it?

I took a long breath in and said, 'You know what I want, don't you? Is it true that you're gonna have my kid?'

She blinked a couple of times and bit her bottom lip. Then weakly, she said,

'Well, yes ... I am pregnant, and ... and, yes ... it is yours.'

I was gutted. I mean I wasn't surprised or shocked or anything; I'd had a feeling it was true ever since Steve had been laughing about it earlier. But I was so ... so what? Disappointed ... angry ... upset? All of them put together. I took a long drag on my cigarette.

You stupid idiot, I thought, and after another quick drag, I threw the butt away with a lot more force than it needed.

Then I looked at Mel. She was trying her best to stay cool, but she was fidgeting with the buttons on her coat and her cheeks had gone red.

'Why didn't you tell me?' I asked, as softly as I could.

'I don't know.' She shrugged. 'I suppose I just didn't see what purpose it would serve.'

'You what?' I shouted. 'You *didn't see what purpose it'd serve,* it's supposed to be my kid!'

Her face changed again and she looked mad. I don't think me putting on a girlie voice when I said her words had helped.

'Well, what is the point?' she snapped. 'It's not like we're madly in love. Or like you're going to get loads of qualifications and a decent job and be able to support us all, is it? I mean, what is your plan? Quit school and sign on the dole? Put our names down on the waiting list for a damp, scruffy little council flat? No thanks. You couldn't even manage to turn up on time tonight, could you? It's hardly likely you're going to be all responsible and reliable and caring. And by the way, there is no *suppose* about it; unfortunately for me, and unfortunately for the baby, it's definitely yours.'

Her words hit me like a baseball bat. I hadn't realised exactly how much she hated me until then, but she'd just made it crystal clear, hadn't she? And she didn't just hate me, she hated everything about me. She'd got me down as a complete loser, and although I didn't like to admit it, perhaps she was right. Perhaps what she'd said had hurt so much because it was too near to the truth. I mean, seriously, what could I have done to help?

But why was she giving me such a hard time now? She'd been alright at the party; she'd been happy enough to be with me then.

But I suppose it'd been different then, hadn't it? Then it was just a bit of fun. Maybe it'd been exciting for her; shacking up with the rough, slightly dodgy, but drop-dead-gorgeous lad, who all the other nice girls wouldn't have dared go near.

I looked at her again, and the look on her face reminded me of my mom. She was thinking that it was all my fault. She was blaming me so she didn't have to blame herself.

Well screw you, I thought; as I'd just found out, the truth hurts.

'So why did you do it then?' I asked her. 'You knew we were taking a risk just as much as I did. You didn't have to do it, you could have said no. But you didn't, did you? You were well up for it.'

She frowned like she couldn't stand to think about it, then she said, 'I was drunk; it's as simple as that.'

But there was no way I was going to let her off that easy. 'Oh come on, you weren't that bad. I know you'd had a few, but you were OK; you knew what you were doing.'

We'd walked away from most of the houses by then, and there was an empty kids' playground in front of us. Mel wandered over to one of the swings and sat down. After a couple of seconds, I followed her.

'Yes,' she said quietly. 'I knew what I was doing, but I don't know what I was thinking. I'd do anything to be able to change things now.' regret

Her voice had gone wobbly and it made me feel bad.

I sat down on the swing next to her, 'I know,' I said. 'We should've –'

'No, you don't know!' she shouted, and she jumped up and wiped the tears from her eyes. 'You've got no idea. It wouldn't affect you at all. I mean really, how would you having a child change your life? OK, if you did end up getting a job you might have to pay maintenance, but apart from that? Nothing. It wouldn't make any difference at all. But I had everything planned: sixth form, university, gap year. Then a job, a car, holidays, a ... family. Having a baby now would mean my whole life would have to change – my whole future. And that's why, that's why ... I'm not going to keep it.'

I tried hard to take everything in. I knew she'd just had a real go at me, but I couldn't think about that then; it was that last bit I had to get my head round.

It came as a bit of a shock. Other girls I knew who got pregnant just had the baby; and yes, I thought to myself, they did put their names down on the waiting list for a council flat.

But as I should've realised earlier, because Mel's life was different to theirs, she might have a different way of looking at things. It wasn't normal for girls like her to have a baby at fifteen. It wasn't exactly normal for the girls on our estate to have a baby at that age either, but if they did get pregnant, then they nearly always kept it – that was normal.

'So, you're going to have an abortion?' I spoke out loud without realising.

'Oh congratulations, you've got it,' Mel replied. Then she added firmly, 'The appointment's already booked.' And she gave me a look that warned me not to dare argue with her.

There was silence for a while and it started to rain. Mel must've decided it was time to go. After a big sigh, she said, 'I know it won't be easy, but it's the only thing I can do. I've thought about it carefully over the last few weeks and it'll be best for everyone: me, the baby and you.'

Her voice had been ever so slightly softer as she'd spoken these words, but then she checked herself and the cold voice and hard stare came back. 'So really, there's no need for you to be involved anymore. Just leave it. I hope I can get away without telling my parents or the school. And I'll certainly avoid telling anyone it's yours if I can.'

As she spat out the last sentence, she had a look on her face like she'd just tasted vodka for the first time.

I blinked and my stomach got tight. I nearly had a right go back at her then. I nearly told her a few things she wouldn't have liked, and I nearly called her a few names I might have regretted. But I didn't; I managed to bite my tongue and I kept my mouth shut.

After a few seconds, she looked at me and shrugged, 'Is there anything else before I go?'

I knew it wouldn't have really mattered if there had been; she'd had enough.

I sort of wanted to say something then, something about being sorry that it'd happened, sorry that she'd have to deal with it all. But like I said earlier, I didn't really do apologies.

'If you want me,' I said finally, 'Gemma knows where I live.'

'I won't.' She shook her head slightly and walked away.

I sat on that swing for ages after she'd gone. My mind was all messed up and I wasn't sure how I felt. I knew I should have been relieved. I should have danced away from our little meeting whistling a happy tune and kicking my heels together from side to side.

She'd completely let me off the hook, hadn't she? She didn't want anything from me at all; she was going to sort it all out and I had to do nothing. A few more weeks and we could both go back to how we'd been before. Wasn't that the perfect answer to a huge problem? I knew it probably was and I was relieved in a way, in a big way.

But there was also a part of me that felt uneasy, and I didn't really know why. I didn't want a kid, I was sure about that. She really didn't want a kid – not yet and not mine, anyway.

I just wished it'd never happened; wished I'd not been so stupid. It wasn't like I didn't know about contraception or anything either. If I'd have had a condom with me I would've used it, some of the time I did. But that night I hadn't, and the fact that it'd turn out like this never actually entered my head. It just wasn't that important at the time. But now I knew I'd been an idiot.

And although I never said it, I was sorry. Sorry for her and sorry for myself. I wasn't sorry for it though – the baby, I mean. My mom was always saying she wished I'd never been born; sometimes I wished I'd never been born – times like this for example. So in a lot of ways the kid was better off than us – it'd never know what'd happened.

It made me think as well though; what if she had decided to keep it? What then? We weren't all going to live together happily ever after, that was for sure. The kid would've grown up with her, I suppose, and it'd probably have been OK. I mean, her mum and dad wouldn't have let it starve, would they? But what about me? Would it have even known me?

As she'd said already, it was unfortunate that it was mine. I mean, what did I know about being a dad? What I'd learned from my dad and my chain of 'stepdads' I suppose, so that was ... nothing.

You saw other dads playing football in the park, didn't you? Feeding the ducks and stuff like that. But that'd never happened with me. My dad had taken me into town and taught me how to shoplift. He'd had his mates round all the time and I'd watched them roll spliffs and get pissed.

If Mel had decided to have it, would I have been any good with it? Would I have remembered its birthday, and been able to buy it stuff? Would I have ever read it a bedtime story? No, probably not. And would it have cared? Yeah, just like I do.

So thank God Mel had worked all this out already and was doing something about it. It really was better off never being born. That way it would never know how shit it feels when nobody wants you.

I was sure that Mel was doing the best thing, and I knew I was getting off lightly, but I still felt messed up inside.

SIX

It was my last term at school, and can you believe it? For the first time in probably ten years, I went every day for two whole weeks. Mr Rogers looked at me funny every time I saw him on a corridor.

'Here again, Danny?' he said one afternoon. 'It's lovely to see you, don't get me wrong, but is everything OK – I mean, are you alright?'

'I'm fine thanks, sir – apart from the fact that Melanie Carter's pregnant with my baby and is going to have an abortion any day now. Oh, and my mother's brought a lunatic drug dealer to live with us. But apart from that, everything's hunky-dory.'

Actually, I didn't say that at all. I tried hard to smile and I said, 'Yes, sir, I've just realised how much I'm going to miss you all when I leave; so I'm making the most of every minute I've got left.'

He laughed, then carried on walking. I watched him and wondered what he would've said if I'd told him the truth.

Because of course the truth was, I was only going to school because of Mel and Karl.

I was happier if I could keep seeing Mel. The baby thing was still getting to me a lot, and I wondered if she might change her mind – not that I wanted her to – I just wondered. Also, I wanted to know when the appointment was. I thought that maybe I'd start to feel better about it once it was ... over. But there was never a time when we were on our own and I could talk to her, and when there were other people around, she made it completely obvious she didn't want to speak. But at least I could see her when I was at school, and I knew she was OK.

The other reason was that I needed somewhere warmish to go out of Karl's way. It hadn't taken him long to feel at home in our house, and as the days went by I felt myself getting more and more on edge. Home didn't feel like home anymore. It felt like somewhere I was visiting. Somewhere where I had to watch everything I did and said; somewhere he controlled and where I meant nothing.

He was always around the house and his mobile phone rang constantly. He could be really foul to my mom if she happened to talk to him at the wrong time, or say the wrong thing at any time.

Lacey tried hard to keep away from him, but she still got pushed around and yelled at, just for being there and doing the things little kids do. I started to take her to Aunty Sam's as often as I could. Sam was sound; she knew what was happening at home and she'd even tried to talk some sense into my mom – but without success. Lacey was always pleased to go to her house, and eventually, it got that she almost lived there.

Sam would always invite me to stay as well. But I just didn't feel like I could. Even though I hated being in the house with Karl, I hated the thought of my mom being there with him on her own even more. And it turned out I was right to be worried.

It was really late one night and I'd been out with Roxi – that bird from New Year's Eve. She'd got my number off one of my mates and sent me a text asking me to meet her. I wasn't sure about it at first – I mean with Mel and everything – but when I told Chris, he said I'd need my head looking at if I didn't. He snatched my phone off me and sent her a message back saying I'd be there.

Right up to the last minute, I wasn't going to go. But then I remembered how keen she'd been in the club, and I changed my mind; well you would, wouldn't you?

We'd had a good night. Roxi was so happy and funny, she just made me feel chilled, and for a bit, I forgot about everything else that was going on. We'd been ice-skating and then I'd taken her home. Her house had been in darkness when we got there, and after she'd checked there was nobody in, we went up to her bedroom.

Oh I'd learned my baby lesson, don't worry. All proper precautions were taken and no tadpoles managed to escape to freedom!

But then we'd fallen asleep. Roxi woke up first, but that was still about two hours later. Her mom and dad had come home and gone to bed, and we had a right laugh trying to sneak downstairs and get me out of the backdoor without anybody hearing us.

Anyway, I was proper buzzin' as I walked up to our house. I had a big smile on my face and I felt better than I had in ages.

But as I went down the path, I began to hear voices shouting, then the dog started barking and there was a loud crash. It was all coming from our kitchen, and as I got to the backdoor, I could tell that Karl was really on one.

I'd heard tons of arguments in the past, and at first this seemed to be no different to any of the other bad ones. I thought about turning round and finding somewhere else to sleep that night. But then my mom let out a real scream, and I opened the door just as Karl punched her in the face and she fell backwards onto the tiles.

'Leave her alone,' I screamed. I ran towards him and shoved him in the chest.

He took a couple of steps backwards, then steadied himself. For a second he just looked at me – I don't think he believed what I'd just done.

'You stupid little shit,' he said quietly, and then he grabbed something off the worktop, rushed forward and swung it at me.

I tried to dodge out of the way, but I couldn't. I felt a hard thud on the side of my head, then he punched me in my stomach. I coughed and swayed with dizziness, but I got hold of the windowsill, and although I was bent double, I managed to stay on my feet.

'Who the hell do you think you are?' Karl snarled, and as I looked up, I knew he hadn't finished with me.

I had to do something quick, so I picked up the nearest thing to me, which was a wooden stool, and I rammed it at him. This time he was knocked off balance and he fell backwards against the worktop.

I glanced down and saw that my mom still hadn't moved. I was scared she was hurt really bad – or worse – and this drove me on towards the bastard who was just beginning to get up.

I really lost it; I shouted and threatened and called him all the names under the sun, and then, when I saw a knife lying on the worktop, I reached my hand out towards it.

But I didn't quite get hold. Instead, Karl grabbed my wrist and bent my arm backwards. I spun around in the same direction to ease the pain, but then I felt myself choking. He'd got behind me somehow and he had his arm tight around my throat. I was gasping for breath and yanking at his wrist as hard as I could, but he was pulling me back so fast, my legs couldn't move quick enough to keep up.

I banged my head hard when I hit the floor. Although I knew I needed to get back on my feet, I just couldn't make myself move.

I got kicked a lot then.

He booted me so hard that my head and kidneys felt like they were going to bust open. My ears were ringing, but I still heard the loud crack as my teeth got smashed together, and my mouth filled up with blood.

All I could do was try and curl up and wait for either it to stop, or for me to lose consciousness. To be honest, I didn't really care which happened first, as long as one of them happened quick.

But nothing did happen that quick in the end. It seemed like a life time went by, and I really started to think he was going to kill me.

But then, slowly, I became aware of voices shouting, and the kicking stopped.

I laid still, tried to clear my mind and get my breath back. I felt somebody get hold of my arm and a man said, 'Are you alright, mate?'

Although, obviously I wasn't, I nodded. Then I opened my eyes and I eventually managed to focus on the man who was kneeling down next to me – he was a cop, and two more of them had handcuffed Karl and were dragging him out of the house.

The policeman helped me get back on my feet and he held me for a few seconds so I could get my balance.

'Where's my mom?' I asked him.

'She's alright, she's in the hallway.'

I walked slowly into the hall and saw my mom sitting on the stairs smoking. One side of her face was red and swollen and tears were rolling down her cheeks.

'We'll have to get that seen to,' she sniffed, and she nodded at the front door; it was all smashed in.

'How did they know?' I asked.

My mom shrugged. But the copper had followed me into the hallway and he answered my question.

'We received a 999 call from a neighbour who said she could hear screaming and see fighting at your house. We weren't very far away.' He paused and looked at me. 'Which was very fortunate for you – you couldn't have taken much more of that.'

I could guess who'd made the call; there was a neighbour across our back who could see into our kitchen from her bedroom. I'd always thought she was just a nosey old bag before, but God, was I grateful she'd made that telephone call.

The cop wanted me and my mom to go to hospital, but we both said no. By the time they'd finished with everything, I just wanted to go to bed. So they told us they'd come back the next day to take proper statements, and they left us alone.

My mom was still crying a lot and I felt like shit; every square centimeter of my body felt raw.

I'd just about made it upstairs and managed to grab a handful of painkillers from the bathroom, when I thought about Lacey. Where was she? At home or at Sam's? I couldn't remember. All I wanted to do was lay down, but I had to check.

I opened her bedroom door and went over to her bed. In the darkness, I had to look hard to see her. I leaned forward – which didn't do my ribs much good – and eventually worked out she was laid on her front with the pillow over the back of her head, and she was holding it there with a little hand at each side.

'Lacey,' I whispered. 'It's me, are you OK?'

'Danny!' she whispered back, and she threw both arms up round my neck and pulled me towards her.

The pain made me gasp, but I couldn't say anything, could I? So with a really big effort, I hugged her back.

'Don't worry,' I said after a few minutes. 'He's gone now.'

And then, thinking I might soon pass out, I crawled into my own bed and went out like a light.

***

The next morning, I opened my eyes, blinked, then quickly closed them again tight. I had a few seconds of peace, then everything came back to me from the night before. I hated Karl. The bastard. The – I went on to silently call him all the obscene names that I knew, and there were a lot.

But then I sorted myself out and focused on the only good thing I could think of. At least he'd gone now. Well, he was out of the house at least, I knew he'd still be around the estate, and I'd have to give that one some thought ... but not now; everything hurt too much to think about it now.

My head felt like I had a set of snooker balls banging around in there, and although I was only taking very tiny little breaths, every single one sent a sharp pain up and down my back and sides. I knew I needed to go back to sleep.

Very carefully, I turned over, and saw a big patch of dried, brown blood on my pillow. I reached up and touched the left side of my head. I could feel a big cut and a lot of thick, gooey blood was stuck to my hair.

What the hell had he hit me with?

I felt like I was swaying and I closed my eyes. I must've drifted back to sleep fairly quickly; in fact, I drifted in and out of sleep for another full day.

When I woke up properly, it was because I needed something to eat and drink. I didn't know if my mom had been into my bedroom since the bust up, but I hadn't seen her if she had. She definitely wasn't the type to sit at my bedside feeding me homemade soup anyway, so I knew I'd have to make it downstairs if I wanted something to eat.

I shivered my way through a shower and looked at myself in the mirror.

I was definitely still alive – and that was a miracle. I had a lot of bruises, but they'd be mostly covered up once I got dressed. One of my back teeth felt strange and sharp and my tongue kept touching it. But the blood had washed out of my hair, and apart from a having a face as white as chalk, I didn't look too bad.

My mom was downstairs, sitting on the settee. The television was on loud, but she wasn't watching it, she was staring hard in the opposite direction. She didn't look at or speak to me when I went in the room, but that wasn't unusual.

'Mom, are you OK?' I asked her.

She turned to me, and I saw a big yellow and purple bruise around her left eye and down her cheek.

She didn't answer me, but after a bit she moved up to make a space for me to sit down next to her – that was unusual, but I sat down anyway. She got a couple of fags out of a packet and gave one to me.

'I came into your bedroom earlier,' my mom said, after a few minutes. 'Lacey was worried cos she couldn't wake you up. You looked awful. I didn't know if I should do something ... a doctor or something.'

'Oh, I'll live,' I said, with a smile. I didn't know exactly how to react to this. I mean, my mom being sort of concerned, my mom talking to me like she cared a bit. Not shouting or having a go. It felt awkward.

After a couple of seconds of wondering what to do, I started to joke around, and I waved the cigarette in front of me. 'You gonna give me a light for this then? Or do you expect me to rub two chair legs together until I make fire?'

My mom handed me a lighter and smiled like she was thankful for what I'd just said. She must've felt awkward as well;

it didn't come easy to her, this caring business.

I was just working my way up to going into the kitchen to look for something to eat when there was a knock at the front door.

My mom got up and peered around the curtains. 'It's the police,' she said. 'They came round yesterday. They want us to make statements and press charges. I told them straight that I wouldn't, but they said they still wanted to talk to you about it.'

She looked at me. Her eyes were big and frightened.

'It's OK, I won't say anything.'

She smiled.

There was no way I would have pressed charges anyway, even without my mom's scared look. Living in the same area as Karl was going to be tough enough as it was, without grassing him up to the cops.

The three blokes came into the house and stood looking at me. There was a tall one, a short one and a fat one. They weren't all police though. One of them – the fat one – was a social worker called Pete.

They asked me a lot of questions about what had happened, and I was really vague and kept saying I couldn't remember. The two coppers started to get fed up when they *realise*

twigged on I wasn't going to press charges, and they were ready to go.

But Pete the Social Worker was far from done.

He said that what the police had seen when they got there was enough for Social Services to get involved, and that I could be classed as a victim of child abuse – me, child!

He wanted me to go to the hospital for a medical examination and report to be done, and for them to take photographs of the bruises and the cut on my head – for evidence.

'Are you kidding?' I laughed. 'I'm OK.'

'Well, I don't think you are, Daniel. You have some *serious* severe injuries and I think you should see a doctor. It's my job to make sure that you're well; that you're safe.'

I shook my head. 'No!' I snapped. 'I'm OK.'

'Well, all right then, but what about your little sister ...' He looked in a folder thing he'd brought with him. '... Lacey?' he said, after reading through some notes. 'Do you think she's safe?'

I thought about it for a few seconds. He was being smart, trying to blackmail me into doing the hospital and photo stuff; he was trying to get his evidence – evidence for what?

'She's fine now that bastard's gone,' I told him. 'I'll look after her.'

He looked at my mom then, but she looked away. 'Is it true that Mr Robinson won't be coming back?'

She didn't answer, so he carried on, 'I'm not sure you realise how serious this is. If he is still here, we'll have to do assessments. Lacey and Daniel's names could end up on the child protection register. Now, does Karl Robinson still live here?'

'No, he's gone,' she said quietly.

'Right; good. You should be aware though, that if he returns to the residence in the future, your children could be considered to be at significant risk, and we might have to take measures to protect them.'

My mom nodded, and after one last go at trying to persuade me to go to the hospital, they went.

Soon after that my mom went out. I laid down on the settee and relaxed. Maybe, just maybe, things were on the up.

SEVEN

After a few days I'd recovered enough to go round to Chris's house. I was dead bored at home on my own and I needed to get out. I knocked on the door and Chris answered, but he didn't let me in. Instead, he rushed out and told me to be quiet. We'd run up his drive and were halfway down the street before he slowed down and started to talk.

'It's our Lee,' he said. 'He's gone right off you since Karl shacked up with your mom. He thinks you must be part of the empire.' Chris laughed, and I joined in. rivalry

'Nah, not me mate. Anyway, he's gone. We all had a big bust up the other night; he got arrested and everything.'

'Oh yeah, I heard the cops were round at your house; didn't know why though. Lee'll be dead chuffed when he finds out Karl's banged up.'

'Well I'm not sure that he still is. Does Lee really care about him that much?'

'Course he does.' Chris nodded. 'There'd be a lot less competition about if Karl was off the scene.'

I hadn't realised Lee was taking his new business so seriously, and I hoped he'd be alright about me when he found out Karl had gone – I mean, I could do without both of them wanting to kill me.

But I soon began to feel better; me and Chris carried on walking, having a smoke and having a laugh, and for a bit it was just like it used to be.

As we went along, we met Gemma. She was walking home from school and she looked worried when she saw me.

'Are you OK?' she asked. 'I heard your mom's boyfriend gave you a right pasting.'

'Oh, I'm fine ...' I smiled. Did she have to be so blunt? I mean, I'd have liked to have had a little bit of self-respect left! But I knew she didn't mean anything by it.

Quietly, I asked her, 'Err ... how's Mel?'

Gemma looked down. 'She's alright, but ... well, do you know about the baby?'

I shook my head.

'She ... she had a miscarriage ... the other day.'

Oh. So that was it then, she'd done it. She must've made up that little story to explain it all to everybody, but that didn't really matter; if it made her feel better, then it was fine by me. I wondered if it'd all gone OK.

I must've looked a bit upset, because Gemma leaned over and gave me a big hug, and Chris said, 'Come on, mate, I'll walk home with you.'

'Nah, you're alright … honestly; I'm fine. I'll see you later.'

***

I was knackered when I got in – I suppose I hadn't recovered as much as I thought. My ribs and back felt sore and I breathed a sigh of relief when I laid down on the settee.

I closed my eyes and straight away I thought about Mel. Part of me really wanted to talk to her; to ask her how she was. But on the other hand, I didn't want to get into another argument or have to put up with her having another go at me. I mean, why go out looking for trouble? So in the end I decided to leave it for now, and to try and make it into school the following week to see her.

I put the telly on and was just flicking through the channels when I heard the front door open. My mom came to the doorway and smiled. I was suspicious, but before I had time to work out how to react, Karl came and stood behind her.

My chin nearly hit the floor.

'It's OK,' my mom said. 'Karl's fine about everything. It's all forgotten about. We'll just carry on like it never happened.'

I sat upright. Can you believe it? She'd let him come back; the psycho who'd given her a black eye, and me a near death experience. She'd taken him back and she was telling me that he was OK about what'd happened.

My heart began to pound inside my chest and I could almost feel the blood rushing round my body. How could she? She'd heard what the social worker had said. How could she put him before me and Lacey?

I started to lose it. I started to feel a sort of mist filling my head, and my eyes stopped blinking. But I fought hard, really hard, to stay in control. I breathed very slowly, stopped clenching my teeth and made my shoulders drop. I sat and concentrated; concentrated on staying quiet and staying still.

'Yeah, no hard feelings, eh?' Karl grinned. He was obviously on his best behaviour, but I couldn't answer him, even if I'd known what to say, I just couldn't have spoken to him without telling him exactly what I thought, and that would have been plain dumb. So I just stared straight ahead.

After a few seconds, Karl spoke again, 'How about a drink?' He winked at my mom.

'We haven't got any in,' my mom said. 'Sorry.' There was an edge to her voice that showed she wasn't totally convinced by the all smiling, all caring new Karl either, and once again I asked myself, how the hell could she?

'Here, nip down the shop and get some.' Karl produced a wad of notes from his back pocket and gave one to my mom.

She smiled and was obviously <u>relieved</u>. She almost skipped out of the front door.

Then, Karl came over and sat next to me – a lot closer than he needed to. I started to get up, but he got hold of my arm.

'Nah then, don't go,' he said. The fake friendliness had gone and he spoke like he was giving an order. 'I wanna talk to ya.'

I sat back down and took a deep breath. I was fairly calm by then, but right uneasy – what did he want?

'Yeah?' I said, trying not to sound too shaky, but also not too clever.

'I was wondering if you'd like to run a few <u>errands</u> for me?'

'What do you mean?' I asked, like I didn't already know.

'Picking a few things up, dropping a few things off. You'd hardly have to do owt really, and I'd see ya right.'

I thought about it for a few seconds – not because I had to decide whether I wanted to work for him or not, but because I was trying to think of the best way to say no.

In the end, the best I could come up with was, 'Nah, it's OK.'

He looked surprised for a second, but then quickly he was sure of himself again and he leaned towards me, almost whispering. 'You'd be daft not to, sunshine. I mean, it'd be a really stupid thing to do, to say no.'

Of course I knew he wasn't going to take no for an answer, and I knew I was crazy to have even tried. He obviously wanted me to work for him, and people like Karl were used to getting what they wanted.

I did have a choice I suppose, but the choice was, say yes, or get my head kicked in again – or worse.

'Alright then,' I said. 'I'll do it.'

'Excellent.' He beamed. 'Oh, there's just one other thing as well.'

I blinked; what now?

'That mate of yours – the one from the club – his big brother's getting a bit too busy; I could do with him going away for a bit. I hear he's out on license and tagged, so if the coppers were to find all that gear in the house, that'd probably do it I reckon. I want you to let the cops know.'

No. No. No, I thought, I can't do that. But it would've been pointless – and suicidal – to have argued, so I dropped my eyes and nodded.

Karl laughed and ruffled my hair hard. 'Good lad, you know it makes sense.' Then he stood up, got a mobile phone out of his pocket and threw it to me. 'Keep it switched on – all the time,' he said, and he went off whistling into the kitchen.

I flopped back and breathed out. What could I do? How could I get out of this one?

I could've told my mom I suppose, but I knew she wouldn't have done anything. Karl obviously had some kind of hold over her and she was scared to death of him.

I could've told fat Pete, the social worker. But then what? A whole lot of rows and fights. And what if my mom still stuck with Karl? Could Lacey end up in care? I wasn't sure and I couldn't risk it.

There was no way I wanted to grass Lee up, but how could I get out of it without Karl kicking off big time?

I closed my eyes and shook my head. What a bleeding mess.

EIGHT

From the minute Karl gave me that mobile phone, it seemed like it never stopped bloody ringing. I was all over the place; going between Karl and his punters constantly. I had no time to see Chris or any of my mates anymore, and when Roxi sent me a text or tried to call me, I always ignored her – she was better of out of it.

I tried so hard to keep Karl sweet, hoping that if I made enough money for him he'd forget about Lee, and leave me alone.

But he didn't.

'I ain't seen no action round at lippy Lee's,' he said to me after a few weeks.

'I phoned the other day,' I lied. 'I told them everything.'

'Well you'd better hope something happens soon, sunbeam, or I might start to think you're telling me porkies.'

Karl paused, then spoke again in his most sarcastic caring voice. 'I mean, it'd be awful if anything happened to your mom, or little Lacey, or even that posh bird you knocked up.'

My stomach felt like it was trying to squeeze its way up through my throat. How could the bastard threaten to hurt Lacey? And Mel? How the hell did he know about Mel? Then there was my mom. He'd hurt her before, he wouldn't think twice about doing it again. I went hot and felt sick.

He knew he had me scared and he loved it. He laughed out loud and was dead pleased with himself as he walked away.

He could be bluffing, I thought? But he probably wasn't. Karl was crazy. He'd hurt anybody and enjoy it. He was twisted. I mean, he could've got any one of his joeys to grass Lee up, but he was making me do it because he knew Chris was my mate – he was showing me he could do whatever he wanted; that he had me backed into a corner.

And he was right.

So that night, I got completely wasted and I phoned the cops.

***

I was dead surprised they did it so quick, and I had no idea what'd happened at first. I only found out when I got a call from a new bloke who used to be one of Lee's best customers. When I met him, he told me all about the raid on Chris's house.

'The coppers had a right old birthday,' he said. 'Middle o' night they turned up, and they found more drugs in their house than there is in Boots. Apart from all the stuff, they got some guns an' all. Lee was arrested straight away.'

'Has he been bailed?' I asked.

'Nah, no chance; not with him already being on a tag. They got their young un and all,' he added.

'You mean Chris?'

'Yeah, that's him, and so I heard, his fingerprints were all over one o' guns.'

I just couldn't take in what he was saying. I couldn't believe that Chris'd been banged up and it was all my fault.

The bloke went, and I wandered around for a bit. Chris could end up doing a long time inside for this, I thought. Both him and Lee had been done before for possession and intent, and from what that bloke had said, the police had got plenty on them this time.

And then there was that gun – what if Lee had used it on a job? There was a good chance he had, and then Chris'd be up for that as well.

I felt right bad about what'd happened. I'd known Chris since we'd been about five or six, and although we hung about with loads of other kids, it was always me and him who really stuck together ... until now.

Some mate I'd turned out to be.

I hadn't aimed for anywhere in particular as I'd walked along, but I ended up quite near school. I went round a corner and as I looked up, I saw a bus stop and somebody I knew – Mel. Without thinking about it, I stepped back behind the wall, then looked around it slowly.

I'm not really sure why I didn't want her to see me – I just felt uneasy about it.

This was the first time I'd seen her for ages. Obviously, after I'd started my new career, I'd never made it back into school. I mean, can you imagine it? Me, sitting in maths answering the phone every ten minutes and making the arrangements, then nipping out at morning break to supply the needs of the local community? I just don't think it would've worked, do you?

So looking at her now, it felt strange. She was talking to this lad and they were laughing. He was older than us but I knew him a bit. He was good looking and he was dressed really well – just like her. He was a right old brain box as well – just like her. I remembered all the assemblies where he'd got loads of awards, not just for exam

results, but for sport and stuff like that —
just like her.

He put his arms around her then and
kissed her.

I just stared at them, and my heart
sank. I don't really know why I felt like
that. It wasn't like I was jealous, well not
about the fact that he was Mel's boyfriend
and I wasn't, anyway.

Maybe I felt rejected? But that was
nothing new; so why should it bother me
now?

What then? What was I feeling that was
screwing me up so much?

Cheated. That's what.

At the risk of sounding like a little kid, it
just wasn't fair. Why should I be stuck with
a crap mother and crazy Karl? Why should
I have to live on a scummy estate in a dump
of a house?

I didn't want to be him — Mel's wonder-
boy I mean — I wanted the chance to be like
him. I wanted to choose whether I passed
exams and got a good job, whether I ended
up living in a big house with a BMW and a
double garage, whether I went on holiday
to flashy places and had a bunch of happy,
clever and confident kids. I wanted that
choice.

I mean, I didn't have it when I was younger, did I? Other people made choices for me then; whether I went to school or not, whether I hung about on the streets at night, whether I had decent meals, a good night's sleep, clean clothes, hugs and kisses ...

The phone rang then. I took it out of my pocket and looked at it – another regular customer. I glanced back at Mel and I thought about her and the kid.

Wouldn't she just love this? Everything she'd said about me had come true. I was a low-life drug dealer – not even that really – a runner for a low-life drug dealer, who'd just grassed up his best mate. I could just see the smug look on her face if she ever found out.

But now I'm gonna be like you, I thought to myself, as I took one last look at Mel and her boyfriend. I can do it. I can be responsible, I can get qualifications, I can ... care. I've just got to give myself a chance, that's all.

I launched the phone into a nearby bush. 'I'm getting out of here,' I said out loud.

There was no point trying to change things if I stayed round here. My mom, Chris, Lee, Karl. They'd drag me back in. I knew I'd got to get away ... but I needed to go home first, just for half an hour.

***

Lacey had been picked up from school by a neighbour and was still at their house. I went to get her and took her straight round to Sam's. I told Sam all about Karl being back and what fat Pete had said, and I made her promise to keep Lacey there. Lacey cried and I hugged her really hard.

'Don't leave me,' she said.

'I'll come back for you,' I told her. 'Honest, I swear down; as soon as I find somewhere to live, I'll come back and get you.'

I really meant it.

Then I went back to our house and got some clothes and stuff. I didn't really know what to take and I had no idea where I was going to go. I'd hardly ever been out of the city before; our area and our estate were all I really knew.

I began to feel right shaky, and so to try and calm me down I helped myself to some of Karl's stuff – corporate theft I think they call it?

I also took all the money I could find in Karl's hidey holes – I knew he'd go psycho when he found out, and I did worry about my mom – but let's face it, she hadn't worried too much about me when she'd let Karl back into the house and he'd sent me out to deal for him, had she?

But I did still worry.

There was something else about the money as well; it was dirty money. Drug money. I was supposed to be getting away from all that. But I wasn't stupid either. I knew I'd need some cash – a lot of cash in fact – to pay for somewhere to stay and everything. Taking it from Karl was the most blameless way of getting it I thought.

I was in the hallway about to leave when I heard voices outside.

'I've been tryin' to get hold of him for the last hour.' Karl was mad. 'He's not answering his phone to anybody, the lazy little git. I'll fuckin' kill him.'

Thank God he'd been angry enough to shout; otherwise I'd have walked straight into him. I dodged into the kitchen as they came in through the front door.

I put my hand on the back door handle but it didn't move; it was locked. Shit, where was the key?

'Nah then, you here?' Karl yelled.

I looked around everywhere ... I couldn't see it. I heard his footsteps and held my breath ... but he went upstairs, and I breathed out.

He was still shouting and I knew by the thuds on the floorboards that he'd stormed into my bedroom.

'I'll break your bleedin' neck when I get my hands on ya.'

Where was that damn key?

Then he kicked one of the doors and made a sort of roaring noise. That was him finding out the money had gone, I guessed, and now he was running back downstairs, shouting at my mom ... and then ... and then ... there it was, behind the kettle – the key.

Silently, I closed the back door behind me. The sound of bangs and crashes came from inside the house, and Karl was still screaming my name.

I walked carefully up our path, and then I decided to make a run for it. I must've been about five houses away when I heard him.

'Oi, come here,' he shouted.

My heart almost stopped, but I carried on running. If he'd have run after me, I'd have been alright, but he knew he'd got no chance of catching me like that. So instead, he got in his car. I heard the door slam and the screech of tires as he spun it round and raced up the street after me.

There was a footpath that went up between a couple of houses nearby and I just managed to get to it. I knew he'd seen where I'd gone, and I hoped he'd drive round to where it came out on another road.

It was getting dark by then, and after I'd run about halfway up the footpath, and I was sure I couldn't be seen from either end, I doubled back.

I had a stabbing pain in my chest and I was gasping for breath. What was I going to do? How was I going to get away from him?

And then I saw it – my ticket out of there.

NINE

The back window was down about ten centimeters. It was an oldish blue Rover and it was parked at the edge of the road – nobody was about. I started to walk towards it, but then some headlights came shining round the corner.

Karl.

I darted back and hid behind a hedge in one of the gardens. The car slowed right down, but then cruised past and I relaxed; he hadn't seen me.

Glancing round again, I checked the street was still empty. Then I put my hand through the gap in the car's window, reached down and flicked the lock inside.

The doors clicked open and no alarm went off. I picked half a brick up off the pavement and got to work quick; smashing the steering column and fusing the wires together. The car fired up straightaway, and as I sat there and revved the accelerator, I felt the power under my foot.

It took a while for me to settle down. But after I'd been driving for a bit, I stopped shaking and I began to smile. I'd done it, I thought; I'd got myself out of there. I'd taken my chance and now here I was, on my way to somewhere and something better.

I gazed across at the bag on the passenger seat and I thought about the money inside it. I thought about Lacey and about how I'd be able to look after her. I laughed out loud.

'Yes!' It'd really happened; I'd done it.

Music blasted out of the CD player. I pushed down harder on the pedal and the dial on the speedometer shot up. Then I played around with the steering wheel, jerking it from side to side, and laughing as the car shook me about.

The road I was on was wide and straight and quiet. It seemed to go on forever, and for ages all I saw in front of me was darkness.

But then I saw some traffic lights in the distance. They were on green, and I pressed down even harder on the accelerator. I was probably about seventy meters away when they turned to amber; stop or go, I thought? Stop or go?

Go, I decided; go, go, go.

I did see them change to red, but I was nearly there by then, and I couldn't have stopped in time even if I'd tried. So I did the opposite; the pedal went right down to the floor.

It was black I think, the other car. I only saw it for a split second – but I did try, I tried to brake and swerve and stop it happening. I honestly did everything I could – but it was no use – by then, it was far too late.

I remember hearing the brakes screeching. And then the wheels locked, and the car slid along the road like it was on an ice rink. I saw the headlights reflecting in the side of the other car ... and then, I suppose ... that's when I hit it.

I must've been out cold for a few minutes, because by the time I came round, the blue flashing lights and the people in the fluorescent jackets were already there.

Straight away, I knew I had to get away, but it took a couple of seconds before I remembered why. The car door was bulging inwards, and although I tugged hard at the handle, it wouldn't open. I climbed across and was just about to open the passenger-side door, when a woman wearing one of the yellow coats opened it for me. She leaned forward and looked in.

'Are you OK?'

'Yeah, I think so,' I said.

'Have you got any pain anywhere?'

'No … well, just my head.'

She helped me get out and had a quick look at my eyes and head.

A copper who'd been talking to some women at the edge of the road came and stood just behind her.

'Nothing serious,' she said. 'But we'll take you down to the hospital and get you checked out properly.'

I looked around, trying to decide which was the best way to run.

But the copper read my mind. 'I'll come with you,' he said, and he got hold of my arm tight.

A loud whurring sound made us all turn round. I have to admit, I hadn't thought about the other car until then, but when I saw it, my legs nearly gave way.

It was mashed up like a Coke can that'd been stamped on. The number plate was laid in the middle of the road and there was shattered glass everywhere.

The noise we'd heard was the cutting gear; they were slicing through the roof so they could get to whoever was inside.

I bit my lip and looked up at the copper. He glared back. 'Bastards who cause it never seem to come off worse,' he said, and I was glad he dragged me into the back of an ambulance and not a police van.

At the hospital, people kept asking me questions. I answered what I could, but I wasn't always sure what they wanted to know. Then they did some tests and took some x-rays and some blood. The copper never said a word, but he stuck to me like Velcro.

I kept trying to think about what'd happened and get it all straight, but I couldn't. It was all messed up.

After a bit, a nurse came to talk to us. 'Danny, you'll be fine in a few days, but right now you're showing signs of having concussion, so we're going to keep you in overnight for observation.' She turned to the copper. 'The doctor says he's not really fit to be questioned at the moment. It'll probably be tomorrow before they give the go-ahead.'

He was obviously pissed off about this, but he smiled at the nurse and said, 'That's OK. We'll just keep him company until he feels up to it.'

They took me to one of the wards, and I laid on a bed and closed my eyes. Straight away, I pictured it; the other car being cut through. Then I heard the whurring noise, and it got so loud my head felt like it was vibrating.

I jumped up. A different cop was watching me by then and he was sitting in a big chair near the doorway.

He looked even more fed up than the first one, but I went over to him anyway.

'Do you know who was in the other car?' I asked him.

'Yeah, a bloke and his young daughter.'

'Do you know if they're OK?'

'He is,' the copper said coldly. 'The little one's in a bad way though; a right bad way.'

I turned around and threw-up.

That night was the longest of my life. I thought about the little girl. Obviously I didn't know what she looked like, and in my mind I kept seeing her as Lacey.

How would I feel, I thought, if somebody had done that to her? I'd want to kill the idiot, wouldn't I? I'd want to break every bone in his body.

I saw the traffic lights turning to red over and over and over again. If only I'd stopped, or at least not been going so fast.

Why did I have to go and that? Why did I have to go and do that to a little kid?

I began to shiver, and I cried. I felt like I used to do sometimes when I was younger. I felt lonely and I felt scared. I wished somebody would come along and put their arms around me. But nobody ever did.

***

Morning came eventually, and the copper who'd come with me to the hospital was back on duty. He turned up just as the doctor had finished looking at me, and the doctor told him I was OK, and I could leave once they'd got my painkillers from the pharmacy.

The copper waited until the doctor had gone, then he turned to me.

'Your mother's refusing to see you,' he said with a smile. 'She says she can't take it anymore, and she doesn't want you back in the family home. Seems like she's had enough of you, Danny, don't you think? Anyway, so we've got to wait for someone from Social Services to come and sit with you while we do the interview, and then, depending on how that goes, we'll see where you're going to sleep tonight.'

He walked off and stood back at the entrance to the ward.

I wasn't really surprised by what he'd just told me. My mom had to choose between me and Karl, didn't she? And for her, that was a no-brainer.

I wondered if she was OK though, and whether Karl was still screwing about the money.

The police would have it by now, the money. I thought about how I was going to explain it all when they interviewed me. I could tell them everything and grass him up big-time, I thought. I knew he'd go mental and I knew he'd get me back for it sooner or later, but to be honest, by that time, I couldn't have cared less.

A bloke walked past the end of my bed just then. He had the local newspaper tucked under his arm, and although the headline was upside down, it hit me like a bullet:

GIRL LEFT CRITICAL AFTER STOLEN CAR COLLISION

The man sat down next to this lad's bed opposite, and he put the paper on the table at the side. I couldn't take my eyes off it. I needed to know what it said, so I got up and went over to him.

''Scuse me, mate, do you mind if I have a quick look at your paper?'

'Help yourself, love,' he said, and he passed it to me.

The first thing I saw was her photograph. She was right cute. She had curly brown hair and freckles, and these big brown eyes. She was wearing a school uniform and smiling away at the camera.

I shut my eyes and had to force them open again after a few seconds. Then I sat on the edge of the bed and read the report:

A six year old girl was left critically ill last night after the vehicle she was travelling in was hit by a stolen car.

Maisie Shaw and her father, Tom, were on their way home after visiting Maisie's grandparents when the collision occurred at the traffic lights on Hillwood Road.

Maisie was taken by ambulance to the city's Children's Hospital, and it has been confirmed that she is suffering from serious head injuries.

The police released a statement late last night saying that they are waiting to question a fifteen year old youth in connection with the incident. It is believed that the car the youth was driving had been stolen earlier in the evening from the Greenfield estate.

A friend of the Shaw family told us, 'Maisie is a very special little girl. She's kind and loving and full of fun. Her parents are obviously frantic with worry. They've been at her bedside constantly, and we are all praying that she'll pull through. It was a terrible accident that never should have happened; the streets just aren't safe anymore.'

It is understood that –'

'Oh, you can read then?' The copper's voice made me look up, and he stared at my face.

'Upset you has it? Well see how you feel about this then; little Maisie Shaw's just died.'

My head dropped back down.

I hardly noticed the handcuffs as they bit into my wrists, and when the copper spoke again, his voice seemed a long, long way away.

'Daniel Watson, you are under arrest on suspicion of causing death by dangerous driving. You do not have to say anything ...'

Also by Kate Hanney:

Watermelon

How far would you go to belong? Alone, rejected, and living in a kids' home, fifteen year old Mikey will do whatever it takes – even if it means running for a local drug dealer.

But as violent clashes with a rival gang escalate, loyalties get torn apart, and the cost of belonging spirals, what risks will Mikey be prepared to take? How will he live with the dangerous and desperate choices he is forced into? And ultimately, can he survive the brutality and betrayal that surround him?

A hard-hitting account of the alienation, conflict and power that rule the streets, WATERMELON will drag its readers along at a breakneck pace. Follow Mikey's authentic voice and compelling narrative as he leads you through his story and right into its fatal, nail-biting conclusion.

Someone Different

Two very different backgrounds; two young people who need each other.

When teenagers Jay and Ann are thrown together unexpectedly, their secret love ignites. But when his world of neglect and youth crime collides with her parents' high expectations for her education and show-jumping success, that love has to battle to stay alive. Will their deep feelings and desperate sacrifices be enough to keep them together, when everything else is pulling them apart?

SOMEONE DIFFERENT is a story of how teenage love struggles to survive when the pressures of parents, prejudice and deprivation get firmly in its way. Set against the contrasting backdrops of an inner-city housing estate and an idyllic country estate, the book takes its readers on a dramatic, compelling and sometimes violent journey, in which the characters' only defence against all of this, is each other.

Did you know ...

a pack of FREE teaching resources is available
to accompany SAFE?

For more information about this, or anything else to do
with Kate Hanney and her books, please visit:

www.katehanney.com

FREE teaching resources are also available for other
Applecore books.

Please take a look at:

www.applecorebooks.co.uk

to find out all you need to know.

Lightning Source UK Ltd.
Milton Keynes UK
UKOW03f0105191013

219307UK00001BA/10/P